MRS PARGETER'S PUBLIC RELATIONS

A Mrs Pargeter mystery

Simon Brett

CRÈME de la CRIME

This first world edition published 2016
in Great Britain and 2017 in the USA by
Crème de la Crime, an imprint of
SEVERN HOUSE PUBLISHERS LTD of
19 Cedar Road, Sutton, Surrey, England, SM2 5DA.
Trade paperback edition first published
in Great Britain and the USA 2017 by
SEVERN HOUSE PUBLISHERS LTD

British Library Cataloguing in Publication Data
A CIP catalogue record for this title is available from the British Library.

ISBN-13: 978-1-78029-092-8 (cased)
ISBN-13: 978-1-78029-576-3 (trade paper)
ISBN-13: 978-1-78010-847-6 (e-book)

All Severn House titles are printed on acid-free paper.

Severn House Publishers support the Forest Stewardship Council™ [FSC™],
the leading international forest certification organisation.
All our titles that are printed on FSC certified paper carry the FSC logo.

MIX
Paper from
responsible sources
FSC® C013056

Typeset by Palimpsest Book Production Ltd.,
Falkirk, Stirlingshire, Scotland.
Printed and bound in Great Britain by
TJ International, Padstow, Cornwall.

Library and Information Centres

Red doles Lane

Huddersfield, West Yorkshire

HD2 1YF

This book should be returned on or before the latest date stamped below. Fines are charged if the item is late.

You may renew this loan for a further period by phone, personal visit or at www.kirklees.gov.uk/libraries, provided that the book is not required by another reader.

NO MORE THAN THREE RENEWALS ARE PERMITTED

A Selection of Recent Titles by Simon Brett

The Mrs Pargeter Mysteries

MRS PARGETER'S PACKAGE
MRS PARGETER'S POUND OF FLESH
MRS PARGETER'S PLOT
MRS PARGETER'S POINT OF HONOUR
MRS PARGETER'S PRINCIPLE *
MRS PARGETER'S PUBLIC RELATIONS *

The Charles Paris Theatrical Series

A RECONSTRUCTED CORPSE
SICKEN AND SO DIE
DEAD ROOM FARCE
A DECENT INTERVAL *
THE CINDERELLA KILLER *

The Fethering Mysteries

BONES UNDER THE BEACH HUT
GUNS IN THE GALLERY *
THE CORPSE ON THE COURT *
THE STRANGLING ON THE STAGE *
THE TOMB IN TURKEY *

* *available from Severn House*

To Gordon and Angus,
our new kittens
(for reasons which will become obvious)

ONE

Mrs Pargeter didn't have any close relations. An only child born of only children, she had lost both her parents in her early twenties. Though deeply saddened, her grief was mitigated by her meeting, shortly after their deaths, the love of her life, the man who became her husband, Mr Pargeter. He, by way of contrast, though he very rarely talked about them, had a lot of relations.

Not only did he not talk about them, he also very rarely saw them. And the reason for such circumspection was that many of his relations had stepped over the fine line which separates honest upright citizens from the criminal classes. Such associations, in the view of Mr Pargeter (who had always had a strong respect for the law), could only compromise the legitimacy of his own varied business enterprises.

So it wasn't until after her husband's much lamented death that his widow first had any dealings with the rest of his family. In fact, the first contact happened some long time after that death. And in a rather unusual manner . . .

One of the hazards of being wealthy is that you develop a magnetic attraction for charity fundraisers. However discreetly and unflamboyantly you live, word gets around that you have money. And, while there are a lot of people out there keen to separate you from that money by illegal means, there are just as many who want to do the same thing for impeccably worthy reasons. And nobody in either camp expresses much interest in where your money came from.

Charity fundraisers are relentless in their pursuit of the wealthy. They pounce on the *Sunday Times* 'Rich List' the minute it drops through their letterboxes and spend a long time trying to find the most tenuous of links between the interests of each name featured with the concerns of their own individual charities.

Their acquisitive antennae are finely tuned to detect any weaknesses in their wealthy prey. For example, the average charity fundraiser would reckon that a well-endowed widow of mature years must, by definition, be a soft touch. But that would be an average charity fundraiser who hadn't met Mrs Pargeter.

She was, however, always open to their approaches. She had no illusions that, whatever inducements their invitations to events might contain, all they really wanted was her money. So if a charity towards whose aims she felt sympathetic asked her to attend a reception or theatrical performance or sporting fixture, she might well accept to check out what kind of set-up it was.

The one thing she drew the line at was charity balls. This was partly because of her single status. The late Mr Pargeter had been a surprisingly neat and nimble dancer, so a ball in his company could be most enjoyable. But attending on her own, submitting to having her toes trodden on by a variety of unfamiliar partners with no sense of rhythm, was not Mrs Pargeter's idea of fun.

Also charity balls always went on far too long. Though Mrs Pargeter had a wide and fascinating circle of friends, few of them were the type who would ever want to 'get up a table' for such an event. And in her experience the kind of people who did want to 'get up a table' had limited charm and limited conversation. So the thought of sitting on the same table with them at a charity ball from seven thirty till 'Carriages at Midnight' – not to mention enduring indifferent food, sweet fizzy wine that wasn't champagne, the inevitable auction and endless speeches of thanks – held little attraction.

In fact, on more than one occasion Mrs Pargeter had willingly paid the price of two tickets for the undoubted privilege of *not* attending a charity ball.

She also had very strong views about the nature of the charities to which she might contemplate donating. Though with a huge appetite for life and a respect for the past, she would never give money to any restoration or maintenance project. It was Mrs Pargeter's view that change was part of progress. If a medieval castle was falling down, that was probably because it had outlasted its usefulness as a medieval castle and would not be missed.

She felt the same about endangered species. Though she probably wouldn't have understood the description, Mrs Pargeter was something of a Darwinian. To her mind, the fact that the world population of Guatemalan dingbats was reduced to single figures suggested that the Guatemalan dingbat was probably not very well adapted to modern life and would be well advised to make an unobtrusive exit from it.

Though the most compassionate of women, Mrs Pargeter's compassion did not extend to the animal kingdom. Friends of hers had cats and dogs that she was perfectly happy to meet socially, but she'd never contemplated owning either herself. She was not afflicted by the pervading British sentimentality about pets. She reckoned there were far too many human problems in need of alleviation before she started extending her largesse to other species.

Which made it all the more remarkable that she was to be seen one evening in early May at a fundraising reception for a cat charity. More remarkable still, given her views on the subject, was the fact that the event was due to include an auction.

TWO

Characteristically, the reason for her presence was compassion for another human being. Mrs Pargeter was generous by nature, but her generosity became even more lavish when it could be focused on people with any connection to her late husband.

Jasmine Angold was just such a person. Her husband too was late (though not as late as Mr Pargeter) and Jasmine was going through the second year of bereavement, which many widows assert is worse than the first. Friends and acquaintances who had been so solicitous during the initial year after the death, who had made such an effort to include the new widow in many social events, seem to reckon that, twelve months on, she should be standing on her own two feet. Meanwhile, the woman herself is facing the bleak and ongoing reality of her partner's disappearance from her life.

Jasmine Angold was not completely on her own. She had a daughter Charley who lived with her – or who perhaps (Mrs Pargeter couldn't remember) had come back to live with her after her father's death.

Jasmine's late husband, nicknamed 'Silver' Angold because of his exceptional skills in dealing with precious metals, had been one of Mr Pargeter's longest-serving and most loyal of associates. They had worked together on projects almost too numerous to count. Mrs Pargeter did not know the precise details of any of these enterprises – her husband had never liked to bring his work home and had always operated on the principle that what people didn't know about they couldn't be questioned about – but she knew he held 'Silver' Angold in very high esteem. It was instinctive therefore that she should extend the hand of friendship to his widow.

Even if that hand turned out to be the one she was led by into a fundraising reception for a cat charity. Mrs Pargeter had been able to tell, from the way Jasmine Angold spoke of the event, how much she wanted to be there. Within a year of her husband's demise, her favourite cat Edna had died just after Christmas, and Jasmine was taking this second bereavement almost worse than she had the first. After an appropriate period of mourning, she had been busy online searching out a replacement for Edna. Which was how she had found out about the particular cat charity whose reception she was so keen to attend.

So, suppressing her own views on the feline world, Mrs Pargeter had arranged for her driver Gary to call in his Rolls-Royce first at her own mansion in Chigwell, then at Jasmine's home in Romford and deliver them both to the Baronet Hotel, Billericay. There she expected to find out more about the charity she was meant to be supporting.

The British, notoriously soppy about pets, seem to become even soppier about pets encountered in foreign climes. And soppiest when the pets in question are cats. On countless flights back to Heathrow or Gatwick from Mediterranean holiday resorts, the cabin staff get sick of hearing sentences beginning, 'Oh, and there was this adorable little cat who was always around the villa and who virtually adopted us . . .'

It's a small step down the slippery slope from that to actually trying to repatriate the creatures to the United Kingdom. 'Nobody else seemed to be feeding her and you just wonder how on earth the cats out there survive the winter. They're all terribly thin.' The thought that this thinness might not be due to neglect but to the animal's ability to adapt to a less bulky body shape in a very hot country does not apparently arise. 'It seemed the least we could do to give the poor little thing a decent home. Oh, there was a lot of paperwork involved, but when you see the expression of gratitude in those little eyes . . .'

Thinking of this kind had led to the setting up of the charity to whose fundraising efforts Mrs Pargeter was lending her support that May evening in the Balmoral Suite of Billericay's Baronet Hotel.

Like many such initiatives, it was the brainchild of a middle-class woman with a very wealthy husband and too much time on her hands. Mendy Farstairs came from one of those families who insisted on giving children silly nicknames which somehow stuck through life. Her husband Rufus Farstairs was an international banker whose aim seemed to be to spend as much of his life in foreign parts as was humanly possible. And, when in the UK, to spend as much time as was humanly possible shooting or on the golf course.

In spite of this packed schedule, he had contrived on three occasions to impregnate Mendy, and once the third son had been sent off to private boarding school, she was at a pretty loose end. Rufus, who had no interest in what she got up to if it required him to do anything other than sign cheques, was happy to fund whatever activities Mendy chose thereafter to indulge in.

The first of these was the purchase and refurbishment of a villa on the Greek island of Atmos. It had been planned as an idyllic bolt hole in which husband and wife could escape from the pressures of life in England and spend quality time together, but in the event Rufus Farstairs only visited it once. That was just after the purchase of the building and he travelled out there simply to check on his investment. On that occasion, because the villa was not yet habitable, the couple stayed in a nearby hotel, the Hotel Thalassa. And thereafter Rufus, having dictated that the place should be called 'Villa Rufus', was quite content for his wife to oversee the refurbishment and decoration of their property on her own.

Their three sons also found the attractions of a Greek island less than riveting, their tastes being for activity holidays with large groups of their braying public school chums, so Mendy Farstairs ended up spending quite a lot of time alone on Atmos. While there she divided her time between patronizing the few other British expatriates and getting to know the island's cats.

Under the illusion that the creatures are interested in human beings as something other than suppliers of food, she reckoned that she had developed a close affinity with Atmos's feline population. Villa Rufus became a magnetic destination for them. Cats infested every corner of the place. Mendy enlisted a local odd-job man called Costas Philippoussis to help look after the growing menagerie, but she wasn't convinced that he had the same instinctive nurturing instinct for the cats that she had. In common with most of the men on Atmos, he was laid-back to the point of torpor. Or, not to beat about the bush, lazy.

As a result, each time she returned to England, Mendy Farstairs worried increasingly about what was happening to her unwitting adoptees while she was away.

For a wealthy middle-aged busybody with too much time on her hands, it was only a small step from these thoughts to the idea of repatriating Greek cats to homes in the United Kingdom. And so it was that Mendy Farstairs' charity was born.

And, in honour of her somewhat lethargic Greek assistant, she named that charity 'PhiliPussies'.

THREE

That evening the Balmoral Suite of the Baronet Hotel smelt of money. Mrs Pargeter was not surprised. She had insisted on paying for both tickets which, at a hundred pounds each, she thought were quite steep for an event where only drinks and canapés were being served. True, the drink was genuine champagne rather than the sweet prosecco with which people were frequently fobbed off on such occasions, but she reckoned the guests would have to drink a lot of it to justify the price of admission.

Both women looked very smart. Jasmine Angold, thin with dark eyes, sharp features and copper-beech dyed hair, wore a dress in silver and gold stripes, bought by her husband in the pomp of his success. Mrs Pargeter's ample curves were magnificently displayed in purple.

Once they had both taken champagne flutes from the trays waitresses were holding at the entrance, they found themselves approached by a woman dressed in a slightly frumpy blue dress which seemed at odds with the designer wear boasted by most of the attendees. It looked almost like a uniform for a nurse or some other functionary in the medical world. On her blue-veined feet she wore brown leather sandals.

The woman's face, surrounded by a cloud of white hair, was innocent of make-up, and had that desiccated, wrinkly look of someone who's spent most of their life under a hot sun. The skin of her arms and bare legs looked as though they had been cured like leather. There was a sweet vagueness about the woman, which prompted an immediate distrust in Mrs Pargeter. She was wary of loopy old ladies. In her experience they could be unreliable. And potentially vicious.

The reason why the woman had accosted them was quickly evident. Pinned to the front of her dress and around the rim of the straw basket she carried was a profusion of small crochet cats in a variety of coloured wools.

'Buy your own PhiliPussy to take home with you,' the woman offered in a wheedling tone.

'Oh, aren't they sweet?' cooed Jasmine Angold.

Mrs Pargeter kept her views to herself. She had long ago adopted the principle that if you haven't got anything nice to say, then don't say anything.

'How much are they?' Jasmine cooed on.

'As much as you want to give,' the woman replied. Her voice was irritatingly coy and other-worldly. 'Though we do suggest a twenty-pound minimum donation.'

Jasmine Angold was immediately rooting around in her handbag. The woman smiled winsomely at Mrs Pargeter. 'Now what colour would you like?'

'I don't think they're really for me,' came the graceful apology. 'None of the colours would go with what I'm wearing.'

She was right. Another colour could only diminish the effect of the splendid purple silk creation she was flaunting.

'What about black or white?' the old woman wheedled. 'They go with everything.'

'Maybe, but I don't want one,' said Mrs Pargeter firmly.

'They are handmade. By me,' their creator insisted. 'I crochet them while I travel back and forth from Greece in the minivan.'

'Oh, do you?' asked Jasmine, more charmed by the woman – and her crochet work – than Mrs Pargeter was. 'Is that when you bring the cats back?'

'Yes, I'm Doreen Grange. I'm in charge of all their repatriation.'

'How lovely,' said Jasmine, once more back into cooing mode. 'Anyway, I'll have a pink one, please.'

'Of course.'

Two twenty-pound notes were proffered. This slightly annoyed Mrs Pargeter. She thought the artefacts were over-priced at twenty. She also suspected that Jasmine Angold didn't have that much money to flash around in this way. But again she didn't say anything.

Having pinned the pink crocheted cat on to Jasmine's front (where it looked rather strange against the gold and silver), Doreen Grange turned back to Mrs Pargeter. 'Sure I can't tempt you?'

'Absolutely certain, thanks.'

With a look almost of pity, Doreen Grange withdrew to accost further new arrivals with the offer of her crocheted PhiliPussies.

To separate the paying guests from even more of their money, the evening was of course to feature an auction. Mrs Pargeter and Jasmine Angold crossed to the table where the available lots were displayed on tiers of small shelves.

There was some very high-end stuff there. Jasmine looked at it rather wistfully. 'I don't think I'll be able to bid for anything,' she said.

Having just witnessed her friend spending forty pounds on a crocheted cat, Mrs Pargeter made a mental note to set up discreet enquiries into the state of Jasmine's finances. Though her late husband had been the most generous of employers and made pension provisions for most of those who worked for him, a few did occasionally escape the net of his largesse. And his widow regarded it as a point of honour to help out any of his former associates who found themselves with money worries.

She herself, of course, had none. She had benefited hugely from the magnanimous provisions of her husband's will. In fact, Mrs Pargeter could have bid for everything in the auction and bought the lot, however high the price went, but she was more concerned as to whether there was anything there she might *want* to bid for. And because, perhaps inevitably, a lot of the objects on show were cat-themed, she doubted whether she'd find anything she'd want to give houseroom to.

The only lots with no feline connections were dinners-for-two at various expensive local restaurants, where Mrs Pargeter was quite capable of booking herself in. Nor did the idea of week-long holidays-for-two in rich people's Mediterranean villas appeal much. She knew that such magnanimous gifts never included airline flights and always involved horse-trading over dates, as the best ones had been taken by the donor's family members. She also knew the aim of all charity auctions was to get people to bid much more than the value of the lots on offer. And that didn't appeal to her. Though the most generous of women, Mrs Pargeter always liked to get her money's worth.

Still, she was there for her friend Jasmine, not for herself, so she must enter into the spirit of the occasion. She took a closer look at the lots to see if there was anything she could make a bid for that wouldn't compromise her standards too much.

There were expensive scarves with cat motifs. There were a couple of cartoonlike paintings of cats with winsomely over-large eyes. There were designer leather cat baskets and crystal brooches in the shape of kittens. Silver cat shapes dangled in the form of earrings.

And boldly dominating the display on the highest shelf, hanging from a plastic branch, was a golden necklace whose design showed two cats slinkily coiling around each other. Mrs Pargeter thought it was hideous.

A view not shared by her friend. Jasmine Angold let out a long sigh as she looked at the artefact. 'Oh,' she murmured, 'isn't that beautiful?'

'Not really my style,' was all Mrs Pargeter could say with any degree of honesty.

Jasmine reached forward and took the weight of the necklace in her hand. 'That's really valuable.'

'Is it?'

'Valuable for the gold content alone, even if it hadn't been made into something so exquisite.'

'Ah. Yes, of course you know about these things.'

'I learned a lot from Silver,' said Jasmine. 'I mean, never nearly as much as he knew, but he did train my eye for jewellery.'

'So how much would that be worth?'

'New, that'd retail in the shops for . . . I don't know. Got to be talking ten grand. Fifteen more likely . . .?'

Mrs Pargeter looked at the necklace again, amazed at the kind of things some people would spend their money on.

At that moment Mendy Farstairs swanned up to them. She greeted Jasmine with perfunctory kisses on both cheeks and shook hands when introduced to Mrs Pargeter.

'Just admiring that,' Jasmine said. 'Stunning, isn't it?'

'The necklace? Oh yes, it was mine. Rufus bought it for me yonks ago. I came across it in a drawer a couple of weeks back, realized I never wore it and thought, Oh well, that can go into the PhiliPussies auction.'

Mrs Pargeter showed no outward reaction. But inside she was asking herself what kind of woman can *forget* that she owns a necklace worth fifteen thousand pounds.

Such speculation was interrupted by a new voice asking, 'Are you Mrs Pargeter?'

FOUR

She turned to see a very well-maintained woman, probably in her early sixties, bearing down on her. Her hair dyed an unlikely red, and dressed in a smart black trouser suit with a lacy shirt, she looked strong and, for some reason Mrs Pargeter could not immediately fathom, oddly familiar.

She admitted her identity to the newcomer, who then posed the supplementary question, 'Widow of the late Lionel Pargeter?'

So unused was she to hearing her husband's first name spoken that she hesitated for a second before answering in the affirmative.

'Ah. You don't recognize me.'

'Should I?'

'We've never met in the flesh, but I thought you might have seen me in photographs that Lionel kept.'

'I don't recall him ever showing me any photographs from his past.' It was true. The late Mr Pargeter had always been economical with how much he told her of his background, of his life before they met. That was the way he always played things. He issued information on a 'need to know' basis, and he had never reckoned that his wife needed to know anything about his former life.

Mrs Pargeter was steeling herself for the woman's announcement that she had been a former girlfriend – possibly even a former wife – of the late Mr Pargeter. She felt strong enough to face any such revelation. Her marriage to Lionel Pargeter had been so perfect, she had felt so secure in it, that she felt equal to any revelation about his past.

But the relationship the woman laid claim to was an unexpected one. Thrusting out a hand to be shaken, she said, 'My name is Rochelle Brighouse. I am your late husband's sister.' Again Mrs Pargeter was too thrown to provide an immediate response. 'He never mentioned me, I suppose?' she went on, her dark brown eyes boring into the violet ones in front of her.

'No, he didn't, I'm afraid,' Mrs Pargeter managed to say.

'No surprise there.'

'And do you have other siblings?'

'No, it was just the two of us. Lionel and Rochelle. Obviously Brighouse is my married name. Don't really know why I kept it. It's survived a lot longer than the marriage did.' She continued to appraise her previously unknown sister-in-law. 'We were never that close, Lionel and I. Interesting to meet you, though. I saw your name on the guest list and I wondered whether there might be any connection.'

At this point a tall man, probably in his thirties, with an exceptionally pale face, loomed over Rochelle Brighouse's shoulder. 'Ah, should introduce you,' she said. 'This is my son Haydon. Haydon, meet your Auntie Melita.'

Mrs Pargeter was almost as unused to hearing her own first name used as she was her late husband's. And she certainly wasn't used to being called 'Auntie'. 'Delighted to meet you, I'm sure,' she said, shaking his hand. And then she introduced Jasmine Angold to mother and son.

'Haydon's a journalist,' said Rochelle.

'More of an author these days, Mum.'

'Oh, what sort of stuff do you write, Haydon?' asked Mrs Pargeter.

'Non-fiction. True crime mostly.'

'Oh, I'm sorry, I don't know anything about that,' said Mrs Pargeter.

'I've done a book about the Krays. And a new one about the Richardson gang is coming out in September.'

'Good luck with it,' said Mrs Pargeter.

'Actually,' said Haydon, 'I wondered whether you might—'

Their conversation would perhaps have proceeded further, but for the sound of a glass being banged and various shushing noises which suggested someone was about to speak.

'And I'm really so pleased to have thought up the name "PhiliPussies",' announced Mendy Farstairs some little way into her oration. 'Not only is it a gesture of support to my Greek partner in the enterprise, Mr Costas Philippoussis, it is also a name of appropriately Grecian provenance. As I'm sure I don't need to tell any of you, a word beginning with "phil-" or "philo-" derives from the Ancient Greek word for "love". So "philosophy" means "love of learning", "philanthropy" means "love of man" . . . and my new word, which I have created – "PhiliPussies" means "love of cats".'

This was clearly a little routine Mendy had reeled out a good few times, and though many of her audience had heard the line before, they still granted it a chuckle of recognition and approval. Those present at the reception were mostly mature females, wearing the kind of dresses with enough fiddly details to qualify under the name of 'designer'. Evidently money was not a problem for any of them. Nor, when it came to their clothes, did taste enter into the equation either.

'First,' Mendy Farstairs continued, 'I'd like to thank you all for coming here tonight. Without your support, PhiliPussies would not exist at all. It is the practical help and financial assistance that you contribute that enables us to continue to do the good work that we do.'

Mrs Pargeter reserved her judgement. She had not as yet given any financial assistance to PhiliPussies, and she wanted to know a lot more about the charity before she reached for her chequebook. Though she had a great deal of money, she was always cautious about where she distributed her largesse.

'There are a few people,' Mendy went on, 'I must single out for special thanks. First of all, Rochelle Brighouse . . .' She gestured across to the woman. 'Rochelle is a tower of strength. She handles all of the advertising for PhiliPussies and organizes events like this evening. She is our fundraiser, and it's wonderful to have the skills of a professional PR person on board for a charity like ours. Apart from the busy day-to-day demands of the agency she runs, but from which she will surely be retiring soon—'

'Never!' Rochelle interrupted. 'So long as I'm still good at what I do, so long as I enjoy doing it, who needs to retire?'

'Well, be that as it may . . .' Mendy Farstairs was slightly thrown by the vigour of the response, '. . . we still enormously appreciate the time that Rochelle finds in her busy schedule to work – completely unpaid, let me say – to help us out with PhiliPussies.'

A gracious smile of acknowledgement from Rochelle Brighouse was rewarded by a ripple of applause.

'The other person to whom I must give special thanks is Doreen Grange, who – wonder of wonders – is actually here tonight. Now the reason I say "wonder of wonders" is that Doreen spends so much of her time in Greece that it is a rare honour to see her in this country. Welcome home, Doreen.'

Mendy gestured to the woman with the crocheted cats who had greeted Mrs Pargeter and Jasmine on arrival. She still had the appearance of a nurturing little old lady who wouldn't hurt a fly. Mrs Pargeter regarded her with increasing suspicion. She had long since learned to distrust nurturing little old ladies who looked as though they wouldn't hurt a fly.

'Doreen, for those of you who don't know – and I can't think there are many – is our coordinator on Atmos. She arranges all the transport of cats from the island back to England – and I'd like to say a big thank-you to her and her many helpers who act as couriers in the PhiliPussies minivans to bring our furry friends to a better life in the UK.'

There was another polite ripple of applause; some of the older women didn't join in but simply beamed. Those, Mrs Pargeter reckoned, must be the helpers to whom Mendy had referred.

'And finally – well, almost finally – I would like to thank two men without whom the whole PhiliPussies operation would grind to a halt. The first is sadly not here because he's back on Atmos, looking after the ever-growing number of cats we have in our sanctuary out there. I refer of course to the man whose name I have purloined for our organization – Costas Philippoussis.'

In absentia, he was offered a little round of applause.

'And the other person who very definitely is here tonight is Bailey Dalrymple!' She indicated a jovial-looking man in a jacket of predominantly green tweed and mustard-coloured corduroy trousers. 'Bailey is of course our vet, whose love of cats and compassion for some of the pathetic strays who make the journey from Atmos back here is exemplary. At his clinic in Leigh-on-Sea, Bailey ensures the safety and health of the little darlings – as well as sorting out their microchipping – and he has been an enormous support to me from the moment I first had the idea for PhiliPussies.

'For those of you who don't know, Bailey Dalrymple and Costas Philippoussis are the only two professional employees of PhiliPussies and, given how much time they devote to the cause, it is absolutely right that they should be paid for their efforts, but all of the rest of the people who keep the charity growing and thriving are volunteers. And I'd like to conclude my few words this evening – before I introduce our very special auctioneer – by asking you all to raise a glass to – not just the volunteers who make PhiliPussies tick, but also the spirit of volunteering, which is so much part of our British culture and which distinguishes us from so many other different foreign countries. So . . .' she raised her champagne flute '. . . to the spirit of volunteering and to PhiliPussies!'

The assembled throng also raised their glasses and produced a murmured echo of her words.

When that had died down, Mendy Farstairs moved on to her final introduction. 'As you know we have very high standards here at PhiliPussies, and when it came to the choice of auctioneer, I went for the very best. I can't tell you how delighted I was when the gentleman in question agreed to take on the role for us this evening. He will be known to you all from the many starring parts he has played on television, but is perhaps most recognizable to us as the crotchety but warm-hearted plastic surgeon Gerald Stickton in the ever-popular series, *A Stitch in Time*. So will you give a warm PhiliPussies welcome to the actor – and so much more besides – Tony Daniello!'

A tall man with suspiciously black hair, wearing a suit only just the right side of sharpness, eased himself out of a coterie of admiring women to take the proffered microphone.

'It's a great honour to be here tonight. I've often—'

But that was as far as he got. At that moment, all the lights in the hotel went out.

Within minutes members of the hotel staff appeared in the Balmoral Suite with torches. They were soon followed by a very apologetic and flustered-looking manager, who assured the assembled guests that everything possible was being done. In a few moments either mains power would be reconnected or the hotel's emergency generator would be activated.

The few moments lasted some five minutes. Then, whether by reconnecting the mains or switching to the emergency generator nobody knew, the Balmoral Suite was once again flooded with light.

Instinctively Mrs Pargeter looked towards the table of auction lots.

The golden cats necklace was no longer part of the display.

FIVE

'The people there were very British about the theft,' Mrs Pargeter confided to Gary. They'd just dropped Jasmine off in Romford and she had moved into the front passenger seat for ease of conversation with him. Gary did not drive exclusively for Mrs Pargeter. He ran his own car-hire company but always made himself available when a summons came from her. And they had a constant battle of her insisting that he should invoice her properly for his work and him continually – and deliberately – forgetting to do so. After all the late Mr Pargeter had done for him, Gary kept saying, he would be honoured to drive his widow around for free. But Mrs Pargeter wasn't having any of that. He was providing a service for her and she was very punctilious about paying for the services she required. Besides, she was very determined that Gary's car-hire venture should succeed.

The late Mr Pargeter had always planned that Gary should work for his widow. A man of great compassion and foresight, he organized future careers for most of his associates. He was an enabler, and directing Gary towards the running of a legitimate car-hire business was characteristic of his generosity. His will even left the driver enough money to buy the first few cars his enterprise required.

Mrs Pargeter had been in touch with Gary very soon after her husband's death. His details, as well as those of many other useful contacts, were contained in what was probably the late Mr Pargeter's most important bequest to his widow – his little black book. In its pages was preserved an invaluable list of names, men – and some women – whose particular set of skills had proved essential to the smooth running of his varied business enterprises.

And after Mr Pargeter's death, this compendium of contacts had proved equally useful to his widow. Many of the adventures she had embarked on, many of the charitable activities she had undertaken, would have been impossible without the willing assistance of the experts who graced its pages.

As a result, Mrs Pargeter kept the little black book as a rare treasure, infinitely more valuable than the wide range of expensive jewellery with which her husband had supplied her (from a variety of sources) during his lifetime. The book was kept in a purpose-built safe behind a specially commissioned portrait of her in the Chigwell mansion, and only brought out when she needed the services of some new expert.

The safe itself was a work of great artistry, and she had actually found the person who created it for her in the little black book. He was listed there under 'Locksmiths and Security' and his name was Parvez the Peterman. ('Peter' was frequently said to be Cockney rhyming slang for a safe, though no one seemed to know the rest of the phrase it was supposed to rhyme with. A 'Peter' is also sometimes rhyming slang for a tan – e.g. 'She'd got a lovely Peter when she come back from Ibiza.' Peter Pan – tan. But as slang for a safe, the rhyme didn't seem to offer any logic. Unless, of course, there was a long-forgotten music hall star called 'Peter Strafe – a Banjo, a Song and a Dance' . . . Unlikely.)

After he ceased to work with the late Mr Pargeter, Parvez the Peterman had become one of London's most respected security consultants. He designed and built all kinds of surveillance systems, and his services were much used by the police, who found he had an uncanny and inexplicable insight into the criminal mind.

As his name suggested, he was of Pakistani origin. His parents had immigrated to Birmingham when he was a small child, and he had taken full advantage of the British educational system. A first-class honours degree in Engineering from Cambridge University had led him to specialize in the area of security, and a chance meeting with an investigator called Truffler Mason at a crime scene had led to his coming under the aegis of the late Mr Pargeter. In that environment he had thrived and developed into one of the country's most skilled experts in the world of safes and surveillance. There was still the slightest trace of Pakistani origins in his voice, which otherwise sounded almost like a parody of an imperial British gentleman.

Though he stocked a variety of off-the-shelf safe designs which would baffle the most astute of cracksmen, he didn't think any of them were good enough for the widow of his late employer. So he devised a completely new electronic system to house Mrs Pargeter's valuables, with an unprecedented series of traps to frustrate attempts to open it. After the keying-in of a wide variety of passwords and codes, the final sesame came from Mrs Pargeter's unique thumbprint.

When he had finished the installation, Parvez the Peterman had grinned with satisfaction. 'Well, Mrs P, your goodies'll be in like an Aladdin's cave . . . except nobody out there's got a magic lamp powerful enough to get into it. I tell you, there's only one person in the history of the universe who could crack that safe.'

'Oh, and who's that?' she had asked.

'A gentleman called "Tumblers" Tate. The only person I've ever met who was better at this game than I am.'

'Did he work for my husband?'

'No, rather the reverse.'

'How do you mean?'

'"Tumblers" Tate worked *against* your husband.'

'Oh?'

'He worked for . . . how shall I put it . . . a rival gang. Known as the "Lambeth Walkers". You see, the East London/ Essex turf was divided up between the Lambeth Walkers, run by a geezer called Knuckles Norton . . .'

The *froideur* which had taken over Mrs Pargeter's expression made his words dry up to a trickle and then stop. 'Anyway,' Parvez the Peterman picked up again, '"Tumblers" Tate is the only person who would ever have posed a threat to this safe, and he's long dead.'

'But it sounds as if you had a lot of respect for him, Parvez.'

'How could I fail to have? He was the daddy of them all. Way ahead of the opposition. Kept inventing new stuff, not just safes and locking systems. There was a special recipe he devised for a lubricant – commercial white lithium mixed with beeswax and pine rosin. It could make any size metal door slide open in total silence – brilliant. And he . . .'

Parvez the Peterman seemed to see from her expression that he was losing her in all this detail. So he turned and, tapping the door of her new safe, continued, 'You take my word for it, Mrs P, your valuables couldn't be in a more secure place. I tell you, Fort Knox has got nothing on this little beauty.'

'Well, thank you very much, Parvez. Now what do I owe you for . . .?'

He held up a hand to silence her. 'Absolutely nothing. When I think of all the things that your husband—'

'Parvez,' she said quite sternly, 'I like to pay my bills. The fact is, you have a rare expertise and your time is extremely valuable. I hate to think how long it must have taken you to make this wonderful—'

Again the hand was lifted. 'Please, regard it as R & D.'

'I beg your pardon?'

'"Research and Development". Something which all manufacturing companies have to factor into their budgets. In making this safe, I was also exploring new techniques. I could either have done that in the laboratory or made a practical application of it by producing a state-of-the-art safe for a client who required one. As you see, I chose to go down the second route. So making this for you was a necessary part of my company's research programme, as a result of which you owe me nothing for it.'

'Well . . .' Eloquent though his argument had been, Mrs Pargeter was still not entirely convinced by it. She always liked to pay her way.

But before she could raise further objections, Parvez the Peterman was off on another track. 'But I also have something else for you, Mrs P. Another product of our extremely inventive research department.' And from his pocket he produced a small black object like a car key fob, except that it did not appear to have any key attached. 'This is called the "Padlock Pass".'

'Oh?' said Mrs Pargeter, intrigued.

'The electronics inside this little thing are extremely complicated, so I will not attempt to explain them. All you need to know, Mrs P, is that if you direct this towards any padlock in the world – even electronic ones or ones with a numerical code – and you press this green button here . . . the padlock will instantly open. What's more, if you press this red button, the padlock will instantly close itself again.' He smiled graciously as he proffered the small device to her. 'And this one is for you, your very own Padlock Pass. Who can say when it will come in useful for you?' Before the issue of payment could come up again, he hastened to add, 'We are giving them to all our clients.'

'Well, thank you very much,' said Mrs Pargeter, putting the gizmo away in her handbag, where it joined a small LED torch and a Swiss Army knife, the basic equipment without which she would never leave the house. 'And, Parvez, do you give these away even to the clients who don't pay any money for your services?'

'We give them away *particularly* to such people. The clients who don't pay any money for our services are of course our most important clients.' He made a little bow towards her. 'Just like you, Mrs Pargeter.'

Once again she thought how blessed she was to be able to call on the skills of someone as gifted as Parvez the Peterman. It was a constant comfort to Mrs Pargeter how her late husband

– and the bequest of his little black book – looked after her from beyond the grave.

It was through the contents of that book that she had made some of her closest friendships. She remembered fondly the first time she had made contact with Gary, how a single phone call to the number in the little black book had been the start of a precious working relationship and friendship.

The driver was a handsome young man, whose background was cluttered with the detritus of failed relationships. In his heart of hearts, despite the age difference between them, he thought that all those failures could be put down to the fact that he'd never met a woman who came near to matching Mrs Pargeter. But he would never have admitted such feelings to anyone – least of all to the object of his adoration.

'How'd'you mean – "very British about the theft"?' he asked, picking up from Mrs Pargeter's comment in the car back from dropping Jasmine off in Romford.

'Well, surely when a necklace worth fifteen grand's been nicked, first thing most law-abiding citizens would do is call the police, isn't it?'

Mrs Pargeter might have excluded herself from that generalization. Though she was undoubtedly a law-abiding citizen, some inbuilt caution prevented her from going out of her way to have dealings with the police. She thought them a fine body of men and women who did a splendid job, but a group whose company she would not for preference seek out. In this, her attitude matched that of her late husband.

'I'd have thought so,' Gary agreed. 'Why, isn't that what happened?'

'No, it was very strange. Nobody seemed that upset – or even surprised – about the disappearance of the necklace. Just got on with things, which is what I meant when I described it as "British". Mendy Farstairs, who was the evening's hostess and who had actually donated the necklace to the auction, seemed totally unperturbed. Mind you, she had forgotten she owned it. Maybe, if you can so easily forget fifteen grands'-worth of kitsch cats, then you're not going to be too worried when they get nicked. No, all she seemed to want to happen was for the evening to go ahead according to plan. She reintroduced the rather unctuous actor who was doing the auction and he did his stuff without the most expensive lot.'

'What was the reaction of the other guests?'

'They didn't seem to want anything to interfere with the smooth running of the evening either. The only ones I heard show any interest in the theft seemed to think one of the hotel staff must have been responsible.'

'Well, they might have a point,' said Gary, who had over the years accumulated a great deal of knowledge about how the criminal classes behave. 'You see, what we're looking at here has to be a two-man job.'

'Oh?'

'One to sabotage the lights, another to make the grab.'

'I see what you mean.'

'So there might be a logic to thinking it was an inside job. I mean, staff members would know the layout of the Baronet Hotel, wouldn't they? So a couple of them might have cooked it up between them.'

'That was certainly what the people I overheard seemed to think. Mind you, I don't think it was logic that brought them round to that opinion, just snobbery. They couldn't imagine that a crime could be committed by "our sort of people".'

'Posh lot, were they?'

'Not genuinely, no. Mostly women whose husbands had made lots of money. One of the most socially insecure sections of the British public, always at the risk of social disgrace or divorce.'

Gary chuckled.

'Oh, incidentally . . .' Mrs Pargeter suddenly remembered. 'You worked for my husband for a long time, didn't you?'

''Course I did. Best employer I ever had. When I think of the patience your husband showed when I was doing my getaway driver course, it was—'

'I don't know what you're talking about,' Mrs Pargeter cut in a little frostily. 'But what I wanted to ask, Gary, was – during the time you worked for him, did you ever meet my husband's sister?'

'Sister?' the driver echoed unenthusiastically. 'No, never met her.'

And he was silent the rest of the way back to the mansion in Chigwell.

It was two days later that Mrs Pargeter rang Mendy Farstairs. The ostensible cause for her call was to say a thank-you for the PhiliPussies reception, but the real reason was curiosity. She was still intrigued by the kind of woman who could *forget* fifteen grands'-worth of jewellery and then be so apparently unfazed by its disappearance.

Her thanks were perfunctorily acknowledged as Mendy moved her agenda on. 'I hope you didn't leave without one of our donation forms . . .?'

'Oh no, I've got one,' Mrs Pargeter lied. And then, adding another lie, went on, 'I haven't yet made up my mind how much I'm going to give.' Whereas in fact of course she had made up her mind exactly how much she was going to give.

'Well, do be as generous as you possibly can. I'm sure I don't need to convince you what a good cause PhiliPussies is.'

Mrs Pargeter did not pick up on that arguable statement. Instead she said, 'I very much admired the brave face you put on the situation at the reception, but you must have been desolated to lose that gold necklace.'

'Not a problem,' said Mendy Farstairs breezily. 'I knew it couldn't have gone far. And in fact I got it back this morning.'

'How?'

'Through the post.'

'Someone posted the necklace back to you? What, in a jiffy bag?'

'Yes.'

Mrs Pargeter's detective antennae tingled. 'Any covering note?'

'No.'

'Any indication where the package came from?'

'No.'

'What about the postmark?'

'I didn't notice.'

'Well, could you have a look now to see where—?'

'No. I threw the envelope into the waste-disposal unit. It's all been ground up by now by the housekeeper.'

The woman spoke with a degree of satisfaction. And once again left Mrs Pargeter confused by her lack of natural curiosity. Or was her motivation something more sinister?

'Oh,' said Mendy, changing the subject. 'Coincidence you meeting your sister-in-law.'

'Yes, it was,' Mrs Pargeter agreed.

'I gathered from Rochelle that you hadn't seen much of each other over the years . . .?'

'The PhiliPussies reception was the first time we'd met.'

'Isn't that rather unusual?'

'Is it?' asked Mrs Pargeter flatly.

'Well . . . maybe it'll be the start of a beautiful friendship.'

'Maybe.' The word was uncoloured by intonation.

'Did you make plans to meet again?'

'No.'

'Ah. Rochelle asked me for your contact details, so maybe you'll hear from her.'

Mrs Pargeter didn't think the possibility required any comment.

'In fact, knowing Rochelle, you'll very definitely hear from her. She's a strong woman.'

Which was an odd thing to say. Not that it worried Mrs Pargeter. She too, when required, could be a very strong woman.

SIX

The late Mr Pargeter had taught his wife about the good things in life. And since she could no longer share them with him, she liked bestowing them on his associates. Which was why she was treating Truffler Mason to lunch at Greene's Hotel.

The venue was managed by a Mr Clinton, known in his former life as 'Hedgeclipper' Clinton. He was enchanted that his late boss's widow always stayed at Greene's when she needed to be in London overnight. He was also gratified that she chose the hotel's gourmet restaurant or one of its private dining rooms for business meetings. When he considered how much Mr Pargeter had done for him, he – like Gary – did not want the widow to pay for anything. But, as with her driver, Mrs Pargeter insisted on being billed properly for all services provided for her by Greene's Hotel. Her husband, she knew, would not have approved of her getting anything for nothing.

Truffler Mason was a tall, lugubrious figure, always dressed in an apologetic light brown suit. He always wore a tie too – he was of the generation that wore ties. And he never moved away from his base without taking a grubby beige raincoat with him. Truffler was pessimistic about most things, but particularly the English weather.

His unique set of skills, though – including tracking down missing persons who were very determined to stay missing, and extracting information from the most reluctant of whistle-blowers – had made him invaluable in the business enterprises of the late Mr Pargeter. And after his boss's demise it was natural for him to redeploy these same skills in a different direction by becoming a private investigator.

He ran a company called 'The Mason de Vere Detective Agency', though the 'de Vere' in the title was pure fabrication. Truffler had just heard from someone that two names on a letterhead gave any start-up a bit of class. He worked every hour God gave out of a rundown, dusty office above a book-ie's in South London, so always welcomed a consultation with Mrs Pargeter over lunch at Greene's.

'There are two things I want you to check out,' said Mrs Pargeter as they sipped champagne and started out on their Oysters Rockefeller.

'Anything for you, Mrs P, you know that. No case I'm working on, nothing that's on my desk has any importance at all compared to doing a job for you.' He sounded as doleful as a bulldog robbed of its bone, but Mrs Pargeter knew him well enough to recognize that this, in Truffler Mason, was enthusiasm.

'I know that's true and I appreciate it very much, but you've reminded me – I've got a bone to pick with you, Truffler.'

'Oh dear, what have I done?' He sounded more desolate than ever.

'It's about the last job you did for me . . . you know, tracking down that Labour MP who hit someone because they described him as a Socialist.'

'I done it all right,' Truffler protested. 'I got a result, didn't I?'

'Of course you got a result. You always do. But the bone I have to pick with you is about the fact that you haven't yet invoiced me for the work!'

'Sorry,' he mumbled. 'I'll do it first thing when I get back to the office.' Then, moving the conversation on to a less contentious subject, he asked her what the two new tasks she had for him were.

'First one,' she replied, 'is fairly straightforward. You know Jasmine Angold?'

'Old "Silver" Angold's widow?'

'That's the one. I'm slightly worried that she may be up against it financially.'

'OK. There's a daughter, isn't there?'

'That's right. Charley. She lives with Jasmine in the house in Romford.'

'And does she contribute to the family finances?'

'I don't know. I've a feeling she doesn't. I vaguely remember Jasmine saying something about Charley having given up her job; can't recall all the details, though.'

'I'll check that out.'

'Bless you, Truffler. Of course, there might be a way of getting the money to them through Charley . . . you know, if Jasmine is too proud to accept charity.'

'I'll see what gives. But basically you want me – discreetly, of course – to find out what Jasmine's living on?'

'Exactly.'

Truffler Mason's sagging face contorted into the nearest it ever got to a smile. No problems there. He'd done a similar job on many of the late Mr Pargeter's associates and their families.

'Next one's a bit stranger,' Mrs Pargeter went on. And she told Truffler about Mendy Farstairs' bizarre reaction to the disappearance of her gold necklace at the PhiliPussies reception.

'May be a wild-goose chase,' she concluded. 'Just seems odd behaviour to me. Probably nothing there, but you know how curious I get.'

'I certainly do, Mrs P.'

'So anything you can find out . . .?'

'Discreetly, of course?'

'Discreetly as ever, Truffler, yes.' A new thought came to her. 'Ooh, one other thing . . . At this PhiliPussies reception I met a woman who claimed to be my husband's sister. Do you know anything about her?'

Truffler Mason's face set as hard as the shells of the oysters they were eating. Just as Gary had done when the same subject was mentioned, he clammed up.

SEVEN

This was something Mrs Pargeter had not encountered before. All of her husband's associates had always been very open with her. Though there were subjects – certain details of the late Mr Pargeter's business dealings, for example – which they were too tactful to bring up, they would, generally speaking, reply with honesty to any question she might put to them.

So to have her two most trusted helpers, Gary and Truffler Mason, refuse to answer her enquiries about Rochelle Brighouse was very strange. She had tried pumping both men for further information, but without success.

All she got from Truffler was the mournful advice, 'The less you have to do with her, the better.'

Which meant that Mrs Pargeter, who usually slept the dreamless sleep of the just, had – by her standards – a rather restless night.

And when she woke up the next morning her mind was still full of intriguing questions. What did Gary and Truffler know about Rochelle Brighouse that stopped them from talking about her? Was there ever a time when Rochelle Brighouse had been close to her brother? And, perhaps most important of all, why had the late Mr Pargeter never even mentioned the fact that he had a sister?

With that convenient synchronicity which no longer surprised Mrs Pargeter, just after nine that morning she had a phone call from Rochelle Brighouse.

'Good morning,' she was greeted in the confident voice of someone who had run her own public relations company for some years. 'It was such a pleasure to meet you at the PhiliPussies event.'

'Well, we hardly had a chance to talk properly, did we, Rochelle?'

'No, you're right, we didn't. But I'm sure we can remedy that in the future.'

'Yes,' said Mrs Pargeter in an even tone which gave no indication whether she thought this was a good idea or not.

'Anyway, not to beat about the bush . . .' Rochelle Brighouse had the manner of someone who never beat about the bush. 'I believe that my brother's death left you an extremely wealthy woman.'

'I can't complain.'

'No, maybe you can't, but I think I can.'

'Sorry? What are you talking about?'

'I'm talking about certain things your husband did during his life for which I feel he owes me.'

'Really? I have heard that such sentiments are quite common among siblings and can become stronger after a death in the family. Having been an only child myself, of course I couldn't really express an opinion.' When Mrs Pargeter got frosty, her syntax tended to become more formal.

'What I am saying, Mrs Pargeter, is that there are certain debts – money owing to me – which my brother left unpaid at his death.'

'Oh?'

'And I feel that you, as his widow, should discharge those debts.'

'My late husband's financial affairs were always meticulously documented. He didn't believe in laxity in such matters.

It upset him to think that he owed money to anyone. But, of course, if you can provide evidence of outstanding debts to you – and the necessary paperwork – I will pass it on to my husband's company lawyers who will deal with the matter.'

'You haven't enquired yet how much I'm asking for.'

'That is true.' Mrs Pargeter didn't add anything else. For one thing she thought it very unlikely that Rochelle Brighouse had any legal claims on her brother's estate. For another, she felt confident that the monies she had been left in various trusts would be more than adequate to settle any minor debts.

'So . . .' said Rochelle Brighouse, 'you want to see some paperwork?'

'I think that's reasonable. After all, I have only your word for the fact that you are any relation of my husband's.'

'Oh, it's true all right. Are you saying Lionel never mentioned me?'

'That's exactly what I'm saying. Until you and I met at the Baronet Hotel, I had no idea that he had a sister.'

'Hm. Well, that's Lionel all over.' There was a strange note of satisfaction in the woman's voice, as if some point had been proved. 'Incidentally, we're not talking money.'

'Sorry?'

'What Lionel owed me, it wasn't cash. Cash would be far too simple.'

'What is it then?'

'Oh, I don't think I need to tell you the details yet, Mrs Pargeter. Funny, can't get used to calling you that. So far as I'm concerned, when I say "Mrs Pargeter", I think of our old mum.'

'Well, I have been called "Mrs Pargeter" for a good few years and I—'

'Oh yes, I'm sure you have.'

'Are you going to tell me what it was that my late husband owed you?'

'You'll see that when you get the paperwork. Which I will deliver in my own good time.'

'Very well, Mrs Brighouse, I will wait to receive it.' Mrs Pargeter now wanted to end the conversation as soon as possible.

But the other woman seemed to be in no hurry. She was happy to linger on the line. 'One thing I should tell you . . .'

'Yes?'

'A bit of advice it is really . . .'

Mrs Pargeter was as close to irritation as she ever got. 'What is it then?'

'Just be very careful if you're going down Epping Forest way.'

'I very rarely do go there. I—'

'There's a lot of secrets in Epping Forest.' And with that enigmatic remark, Rochelle Brighouse decided to end the conversation.

The call from Rochelle had unsettled Mrs Pargeter further, but it was not in her nature to remain unsettled for long. As the day progressed her irritation gave way to curiosity, and by the evening even that had been replaced by her customary benign thoughts.

So it was with some surprise that the following morning, when she was half-listening to the radio news, she heard this announcement:

'The identity of a woman's body which was found last night in a shallow grave in Epping Forest has been confirmed. It was that of a seventy-seven-year-old charity worker called Doreen Grange. Essex Constabulary have launched a murder enquiry.'

EIGHT

Though Mrs Pargeter greatly disliked crocheted cats, she didn't think their manufacture was sufficient provocation for murder. And, like the police, she felt sure it was murder they were dealing with. Suicides may deal efficiently with the actual process of killing, but they rarely manage to bury themselves after their deaths in shallow graves in Epping Forest (which is, incidentally, London's go-to destination for the burying of bodies in shallow graves).

Of course Mrs Pargeter knew virtually nothing about the late Doreen Grange, nor indeed the circumstances of her death. But the bizarre synchronicity of recent events had ignited her curiosity.

And once Mrs Pargeter's curiosity had been ignited, it prompted a constant desire for more fuel, in the form of information.

So when Truffler Mason rang her with an update on Jasmine Angold's finances (in a bad state), it was natural for her to move quickly on to the subject of Doreen Grange. 'Do you know anything about her death?'

'Why should I, Mrs P?'

'Well, you've got very good contacts.'

'That's as maybe, but it doesn't mean I know the SP on every crime that's committed anywhere.' He sounded more doom-laden than ever.

'No, I'm sorry, but I thought you might possibly know someone who'd have access to that kind of information.'

'Ah, now, Mrs P, you're asking a completely different question. Yes, indeed, there is someone I know who might be able to provide just the information we need.'

The arrangement was to meet in a pub in Harlow at the end of the working day. The pub was an anonymous concrete slab, to which no amount of dark wood panelling, plush red velvet seats and coach lamps could give any atmosphere of conviviality.

Not that it wasn't full. As Mrs Pargeter and Truffler Mason entered, conversation was almost drowning out the Muzak. Truffler cautiously inhaled the air. 'You know what?' he said, as if announcing the imminent end of the world, 'this is a coppers' pub.'

Mrs Pargeter couldn't have made that deduction. There were few uniforms on display, but she trusted Truffler's intuition. He had very highly tuned antennae for such things. Long experience had taught him to sniff out police presence at a hundred yards. In Mrs Pargeter's blameless life, such skills had never been required.

'But I thought you said your contact was in the police.'

'He is. Bobby the Bill – that's what we call him. His real name's Robert McPherson. But in fact he got his nickname before he joined the police.'

'Oh?'

'Yeah, it was because of his ability to extract payment of bills from reluctant debtors. Dead good at that he was. Once he got started on them, people coughed up real quick. Anyway, the nickname turned out to be very suitable after he changed careers. He started training for the Force the minute he stopped working for your old man.'

'Then why would he want us to meet in a coppers' pub?'

'I don't know.'

'Do you think it could be some kind of trap?'

Truffler Mason firmly shook his long, horse-like head. 'No way. Bobby the Bill's as straight as a lollipop lady's lollipop. If he fixed for us to meet here, he must've had his reasons.'

At that point they saw the object of their discussion. A thickset man, whose shaven head fitted into his torso without the intervention of a neck, rose from a corner table and waved them across. Introductions having been made, he insisted on buying the first round. Truffler Mason asked for a pint of Adnam's, and Bobby the Bill reckoned he was ready for a second of those. Mrs Pargeter, deciding this wasn't the sort of pub where she'd get a vodka Campari, went for a gin and tonic.

When they were all at the table and she was sipping what was clearly a double G & T, Bobby the Bill began to talk about the late Mr Pargeter and what an honour it was to meet his widow. 'I heard so much about you when we was working together, and now I meet you in the flesh I see he didn't exaggerate one little bit.'

Accepting the compliment, Mrs Pargeter smiled gracefully.

'He was such a great guy to work for, your husband. Taught me everything I knew. How to stop rowdy people being rowdy, how to get information out of the quiet ones, how to be alert to conflicts what people're trying to hide, how to recognize when people are up to some under-the-counter stuff . . . Oh, I may have had some natural aptitude for that kind of work, but it was Mr Pargeter who brought it out of me, kind of "nurtured my talents", you could say.

'And then, towards the end of his life, he done something I would never have believed possible. He actually *advised* me that when I stopped working for him I should go into the police force. Imagine that – *advising* me to become a copper. Someone who'd done what your husband had done all his life actually *recommending* I should go over to the other side. I mean, it's—'

'I'm sorry,' said Mrs Pargeter, innocence glowing from her violet eyes, 'but I'm afraid I don't know what you're talking about.'

Bobby the Bill looked puzzled, but Truffler quickly came in with the explanation. 'Mrs Pargeter doesn't know everything about what her husband done.'

'Oh?'

Truffler spelled out the guiding rule of the late Mr Pargeter's life. 'He was always a great believer in the principle of "need to know". So what you didn't need to know you didn't know. That way you could never be made to stand up in court and talk about it.'

Comprehension slowly dawned on the policeman. 'Because you didn't know?' he suggested.

'Exactly that, Bobby,' said Truffler.

'Ah. Gotcha.' He beamed at Mrs Pargeter. 'Anyway, all I'm saying is that I'm really grateful to your husband because he, kind of, give me that career advice . . . you know, he reckoned my skillset was dead right for me to join the Bill, so that's what I done. On his part it was pure . . . what's that posh word for when someone does something for someone else what doesn't do them any good? "Aluminium", is it?'

'"Altruism",' suggested Mrs Pargeter gently.

'Yeah, that's the one. Anyway, your old man, he was full of that.' She nodded fond agreement. 'So, going against all his instincts, he actually pushed me into the police force. Not thinking of himself at all.'

'Erm,' Truffler interposed. 'He was thinking of himself a bit.'

'How'd you mean?'

'Well, sometimes you did give him some useful information, didn't you? Like secret police information?'

'Ye-es,' Bobby the Bill conceded. 'But only because I knew he'd use it in the right way.'

'Of course,' Truffler agreed reassuringly.

Mrs Pargeter was feeling uncharacteristically ill at ease. Though her respect for the police, men and women who did a very boring job with occasional efficiency, remained undiluted, she still never quite relaxed in their company. So being in a pub where every vista was peopled by coppers was not her idea of fun.

'Are you sure that meeting in here is a good idea?' she asked Bobby the Bill. 'Isn't there a great risk of our being overheard?'

'No,' he assured her airily. 'Everyone's talking so loud in here no one can hear a thing. Anyway, cops always stop listening when they've got a drink inside them.' He took a long swig from his second pint. 'I know I do.'

Mrs Pargeter didn't find much comfort in his words. 'If we could perhaps get on with what we came here for,' she urged.

'Yes, of course. Now what I done before you arrived, is to slip a couple of folders on to the shelf under this table, right?'

Truffler Mason reached forward and touched cardboard. 'Right.'

'Now you take them.'

'OK. Do you want me to take them so's people can see what I got?'

'Yes, sure. More witnesses the better.'

'Right.' The private investigator held up what he'd found, very conspicuously.

'Right now, Truffler, what you got there is two folders, isn't it?'

'Yes.'

'Blue one and a red one. Red one's got all the guff on Doreen Grange's murder. Now what I want you to do—'

But Bobby the Bill was prevented from further talk by a sudden quietening in the room. The assembled coppers all turned towards the door at the appearance of a tall man in a dark blue uniform with lots of gold braid on it.

'Don't stand on ceremony with me,' he announced with forced joviality. 'I'm just coming to have a pint with the boys.'

His request had little effect on the silence in the bar. Mrs Pargeter looked across interrogatively to Bobby the Bill. 'Chief Constable,' he mouthed back. The information did little to diminish her level of discomfort.

And it mounted considerably when the Chief Constable came straight across to their table. He clapped Bobby the Bill on the shoulder and said heartily, 'Keeping up the good work, I see, McPherson.'

'Doing my best, sir.'

The Chief Constable favoured Mrs Pargeter and Truffler Mason with a beaming smile. 'You're working with top-notch talent, with McPherson here,' he said. 'Just so's you know that. And I would like to say how much we in the Force appreciate people like you. You make our job a lot easier.'

And with that he was across the room, showing his common touch by asking the barmaid what bitters she had on offer.

'It's the red file we take?' Truffler asked for confirmation.

'That's it. All the info on the Doreen Grange case is in there.'

'Well, perhaps we'd better be moving,' said Mrs Pargeter with some urgency.

'Oh, before you do, though,' said Bobby the Bill, 'you hand that blue file across to me.'

'OK.'

'But do it very obviously, Truffler. In fact, if you could drop it as you're doing so and pick it up, then everyone'll see what you're doing.'

Truffler Mason did exactly as instructed. He acted so clumsily that not a copper in the pub could have missed what was going on.

'What was all that about?' asked Mrs Pargeter as they sat in Gary's limousine on the way back to Chigwell. 'What the Chief Constable said, and all that business with the file?'

'Ah well, you see, Mrs P, that was why Bobby the Bill chose to meet in that pub.'

'Why? It was full of coppers.'

'Yes, but they all thought we was narks.'

'What?'

'Police informers.'

'I know what a nark is, Truffler,' she responded with uncharacteristic asperity.

'They thought we was giving information to Bobby the Bill, not the other way round.'

'So that's why the Chief Constable thanked us for making their job easier?'

'Exactly.'

'Huh,' said Mrs Pargeter.

And she was silent all the way back to her mansion in Chigwell, deeply offended that anyone might have mistaken her for a police informer. To her mind, police informers were criminals, and she had never been one of those.

NINE

B obby the Bill had done a good job. As Truffler spread the papers from the red folder over Mrs Pargeter's sitting-room table, he observed that they now had as much information on Doreen Grange's murder as the official investigating team did.

'About time,' said Mrs Pargeter. 'It's shocking how uncommunicative the police can be about ongoing enquiries. They don't think. Their attitude puts the average amateur sleuth at a considerable disadvantage. At least with this lot—' she gestured to the documents – 'we start on a level playing field.'

They read through everything with great attention. Truffler made notes in a spiral-topped reporter's notebook. (He liked traditional methods; though he did own a laptop, he only used it when he had absolutely no alternative.)

It turned out that Doreen Grange's permanent home was on the Greek island of Atmos, where she spent all of her time and energy working unpaid for PhiliPussies. She was seventy-seven years old and lived comfortably on a generous Civil Service pension. Every couple of months she came back to England, being driven in a minivan full of cats that were about to be rehabilitated. When she made these trips she stayed with her sister Flora Grange in Rayleigh, Essex. Neither sister had ever married.

Her postmortem revealed that the cause of death had been strangulation by a tartan dog lead, which was still in place around her neck when her body was found. Time of death was estimated to have been in the small hours of the same day. The assumption was that Doreen Grange had not been killed at the location where she was buried. Further investigation was required, but it was thought likely that she had been driven in a vehicle from the scene of the crime to Epping Forest. Some threads found on her clothing would need further analysis, but looked very much as if they came from the carpeting in a car boot.

The attempt to bury her had been half-hearted. The grave was very shallow, and whoever dug it could not have expected the body to remain undiscovered for long, particularly as it was quite near one of Epping Forest's main car parks. A favourite area for dog-walkers. And as regular readers of the newspapers know, dog-walkers constitute one of the sections of the population most likely to discover dead bodies.

The police had interviewed Flora Grange at her home in Rayleigh. She told them that the evening before her death Doreen had retired to bed at about ten o'clock. Neither sister kept late hours. There had been nothing untoward in Doreen's behaviour. She did not appear to be upset, frightened or nervous. Her only complaint was about the coldness of Essex in May, when compared to sunny Greece.

Flora Grange had not been aware of any disturbance during the night, but then that was no surprise. Her hearing was very poor and she always removed her hearing aids when she went to bed. She said that a herd of elephants could have stomped through the house during the night and she wouldn't have been aware of a thing. The first indication she'd had that anything was wrong was when she found Doreen's bedroom empty the following morning.

Inspecting the premises, the police found that the bed in Doreen's room had been slept in. There were no signs of forced entry, no evidence of any violence having taken place and no suicide note. The assumption had to be that Doreen Grange had left the house voluntarily in the middle of the night.

Checking recent calls on her mobile phone (which was found with her body) revealed nothing unexpected. All had been related to the activities of PhiliPussies. On the last day of her life she had spoken to Mendy Farstairs, Rochelle Brighouse and the vet Bailey Dalrymple. The one international call she'd made was to Greece. Ringing the number revealed that it belonged to the neighbour on Atmos who was looking after Doreen's own personal pet cats while she was away.

And that was as far as the official police investigation had got.

'Very helpful,' said Mrs Pargeter. 'You hear lots of criticism of the police these days, but there are some basic things they do very well. And they've even provided us with the address for our next step.'

'Next step?' repeated a puzzled Truffler Mason.

'Well, obviously we go and visit Flora Grange. She's the only lead we've got.'

'True,' he agreed dolefully.

'And do you think Bobby the Bill will provide us with more information as he gets it?'

'Course he will. He's as honest as the day is long, Bobby. The minute the police get any kind of breakthrough, he'll pass it on to us.'

'Good.' Mrs Pargeter was silent for a moment. 'I'd prefer it if we found some other way of getting the stuff.' The unease generated by being in a coppers' pub had not left her.

'Yeah, we can sort something out, no problem.'

'Excellent. Though it is quite comforting to know that we'll be up to speed with everything the police are investigating.'

'It is indeed. And when they find out whodunit, we'll be the first to know.'

'Oh, I don't think so.'

'Wodja mean?'

'I mean that we'll find out whodunit long before the police do, won't we, Truffler?'

'Of course we will, Mrs P.'

TEN

Flora Grange's house was an inoffensive suburban semi, only differentiated from the others in the road by its lime green front door. When Mrs Pargeter had phoned, using the number so helpfully (if unwittingly) supplied by the police, the woman who'd answered had been more than happy to talk about her sister.

'The fact is,' she said, once they were all settled in her very suburban front room, 'that I could never stand Doreen. I know they always say one shouldn't speak ill of the dead, but in her case it's very difficult not to.'

Mrs Pargeter wondered whether this was just natural antipathy between two sisters, or a reaction against some criminal behaviour perpetrated by Doreen Grange. On brief acquaintance the latter scenario seemed unlikely, but Mrs Pargeter knew well how often evil lurked behind the most innocent of exteriors.

'Difficult for anyone not to?' she asked Flora. 'Or just for you?'

'Well, it was particularly difficult for me because I spent more time with the cow. She was there when I was born and I've spent most of my life trying to get shot of her.'

Mrs Pargeter was struck immediately by the contrast between the two sisters, which expressed itself both in their manner and their clothes. There was nothing nurse-like in Flora Grange's spangly silver top and red leather trousers. The black stilettos too could not have been more different from Doreen Grange's sandals.

Flora had implied that she was younger than her sister, and from her looks the age difference could have been as much as fifteen years. Whereas Doreen's face looked as if it had never been touched by make-up, Flora's was caked over with the stuff. But it had been very skilfully applied, even down to the luxuriant false eyelashes. Though Mrs Pargeter reckoned

she must be older, Flora Grange could easily have passed for
late fifties.

Flora's behaviour, too, was nothing like her older sister's.
Whereas Doreen's voice had a coy, wheedling tone to it, Flora's
was direct and abrasive. She sounded as if she were afraid of
nothing and used to getting her own way.

Her words about her sister – 'I've spent most of my life
trying to get shot of her' – might have been interpreted by
some amateur sleuths as a confession of murderous intent, but
Mrs Pargeter was too canny to take them that way. In her
experience, genuine murderers were much more careful with
their words. Flora Grange's very lack of caution pointed
towards her innocence.

'I gather,' Mrs Pargeter said, 'that you have been interviewed
by the police . . .?'

'Yes, and a right load of useless tossers they turned out to be.'

'They presumably asked you questions about your sister?'

'Of course they did. What else are they going to ask me
about?'

'And did you express your, erm, lack of affection for Doreen
as forcibly as you have to us?'

'No, of course I didn't. For them I did the full grieving
sister routine. I even managed to produce some tears. That's
why it's such a relief to be able to talk to you. Because you
have no official role in the enquiry.'

'That's true. What I can't understand, Flora . . . I may call
you "Flora", may I?

'Sure.'

'Well, what I can't understand is why, given how much you
disliked your sister, you let her stay with you every time she
came to England.'

'I couldn't avoid it.'

'How do you mean?'

'Doreen had certain information about me which she threatened to disclose to the police if I didn't do as she told me to.'

'Blackmail?'

'That's what it amounted to, yes.'

'Now, I'm not about to ask you what that information was . . .'

'Just as well, because I wouldn't tell you.'

'I didn't think you would. What I would like to know, though, is why you hated Doreen so much? Was it just sibling rivalry, two girls close in age and—'

'Oy!' Flora interrupted. 'We weren't that close in age! Now every newspaper in the country is broadcasting the fact that Doreen was seventy-seven, how old are people going to think I am? There was a very big age gap between us. Different fathers, you see. Our mother married twice. I think I must have been an accident. I don't think she had planned to start another family so late in life.'

'So . . .' Mrs Pargeter dared to put the question, 'how old are you, Flora?'

'Fifty-five,' the woman lied, without a hint of a blush.

'Fine. And can I ask again why you disliked your sister so much?'

'Oh, she was just so self-righteous. A prig. Always doing good works. It got up my nose. Why couldn't she show a bit of natural selfishness like the rest of us? I think it was because Doreen was so bloody good all the time that I deliberately went off the rails. I was trying to get some reaction out of her, something other than patronizing pity. But it never worked. She remained the toffee-nosed do-gooder she had been since I first became aware of her. God, she drove me to distraction.'

'I'm sure she did,' said Mrs Pargeter with a degree of sympathy. Her very brief acquaintance with Doreen had prompted the same reaction in her. The thought of having to endure that pious self-righteousness for years . . . yes, she could see Flora's point. But no time for that, she needed to get on with the investigation. 'And had she always liked cats?'

'Oh yes. Our family home was full of the horrid little beasts. It wasn't just Doreen who liked them, it was my parents too. They certainly showed much more affection to the cats than they ever did to me. I loathe the creatures – scratching everything in sight, yowling all the time, dragging dead wildlife into the house. Horrid things! And Doreen was always bringing more of the little monsters into the UK.'

'Did she ever have any with her when she came here to stay with you?'

'No, she did not! That was one thing I would not put up

with. I drew the line there. No, when she comes back to England the cats get delivered straight to the vet.'

'Would that be Bailey Dalrymple?'

'Yes, I think that was the name she mentioned. I've never met him. But I made it clear to Doreen that I wouldn't have any cats in my house. I am actually allergic to them. I start wheezing if I go within a hundred yards of one. So Doreen wouldn't dare bring one into the house. I made that clear to her. They went straight to some clinic in Leigh-on-Sea. Mind you, Doreen still always reeks of the animals; everything she wears is covered with cats' hairs. The minute she comes into the house, my eyes puff up and my nose streams. My sister is just so thoughtless. She always has been. Like lots of do-gooders, she is totally insensitive to the needs of others. I can remember when she was about seven years old, she—'

Clearly Flora Grange could have gone on in this vein for some time, so Mrs Pargeter interrupted her flow. 'Could we just go back to the last time you saw her?'

'If you want to.'

'According to the information we have . . .'

'And where, may I ask, did you get that information from?'

Mrs Pargeter looked at Truffler Mason for guidance. 'A variety of sources,' he said judiciously. 'We private investigators are a bit like journalists – never say where we got stuff from.'

Flora Grange did not seem to be put out by this, so Mrs Pargeter went on, 'We were told that you both retired to bed early . . . about ten, is that right?'

'Doreen went to bed at ten. She always was a wet blanket, terrible party-pooper. She had no relish for *life*,' Flora concluded flamboyantly.

'Unlike you?'

'Very definitely unlike me. I've always believed in living life to the full, draining its dregs.'

'So you didn't go to bed at ten?'

Flora Grange looked at Mrs Pargeter slyly. 'I didn't say that. The question you should really be asking is who I went to bed *with*.'

'Oh?'

'Sex never featured much in Doreen's life. I'm pretty sure she was a virgin when she died.'

'Whereas you, on the other hand . . .' suggested Mrs Pargeter.

Her appeal to the woman's vanity had just the right effect. 'I, on the other hand, have always been extremely highly sexed. And extremely attractive to men.'

'Congratulations,' murmured Mrs Pargeter. 'So who was the lucky man that night?'

'I'm not going to tell you his name.'

'Fine.'

'He's a local lad. Does a bit of gardening and other services for me.' Flora Grange was relishing the ambiguity of her words. She fancied herself in the role of cougar.

'So are you saying,' asked Truffler, 'that this young man might be a useful witness, that he might have seen what had happened to your sister?'

'Good Lord, no. He was only with me half an hour. I call him when the need arises and he goes when I've had what I want out of him. When he left we could both hear Doreen snoring. He commented on it. She always did snore. God, when we shared a bedroom, the number of nights she used to keep me wide awake you wouldn't believe.'

'I'm surprised,' said Mrs Pargeter, 'that you could hear her snoring the other night.'

'Why's that?'

'Because I thought you wore hearing aids and took them out when you went to bed.'

'No, of course I don't,' Flora snapped. 'Do I look the age of someone who needs hearing aids?'

'Our information,' says Truffler, 'suggests that you did wear hearing aids. Or that you said you wore hearing aids.'

'No, that's just something I told the police.' She looked at her two visitors with renewed respect. 'How did you know that? The only people I told that to was the police.'

'I have my ways of finding things out,' said Truffler loftily, 'but of course I never reveal my sources.'

'You're good,' said Flora Grange with grudging admiration. 'But when I tell you some of the things Doreen used to do to me when I was a small child you'll—'

Another interruption was called for. Mrs Pargeter felt that they'd probably got all the information they were likely to get from Flora Grange. Though she could clearly go on at inordinate length about the iniquities of her sister.

'Sorry to stop you, but, Flora, can you think of any person who might have wanted to murder Doreen?'

'Anyone who had met her, I would imagine,' came the predictable reply.

ELEVEN

T he next morning Mrs Pargeter and Truffler Mason were sitting in Erin Jarvis's front room. No one who had been there when it was the office of her late father 'Jukebox' Jarvis (so called because he 'kept the records') would have recognized the place. In his day a spaghetti chaos of snaking wires had spread across the floor, joining up a junkyard of desktop computers, monitors, printers and surveillance equipment. But in spite of what 'Jukebox' Jarvis himself regarded as a nod to modernity, most of his record-keeping was still contained in dusty cardboard boxes from which file cards, yellowed and flimsy with age, spilled out to join the general chaos of the floor.

But during his final illness the archivist had worked closely with his daughter to explain his complex filing methods, and soon after his death Erin had completed the task of digitizing every last card. For her the time spent working with 'Jukebox' had been extraordinarily precious. In the last months of his life the two of them, never particularly close before, had formed a bond which would sustain Erin for as long as she might live.

And now the only sign that the minimal front room might be any kind of office was the slim laptop that sat on Erin Jarvis's glass-topped table.

But whether employing 'Jukebox' Jarvis's antiquated system or his daughter's cutting-edge modern methods, one thing remained constant. Any information, even the tiniest detail, about the history of the late Mr Pargeter's business activities could be summoned up instantly.

Once she had supplied her guests with coffee from the state-of-the-art Italian machine, Erin said, 'I'm sorry to drag you over here, but I thought it might be easier to explain what's been going on face to face.'

'No worries, dear,' said Mrs Pargeter. 'It's a great pleasure to see you again.'

'You too, Mrs P. And you of course, Truffler.'

His sagging face twisted into the grimace which was the nearest he ever got to a smile. 'Lovely to see you too, Erin. As ever.'

Truffler Mason, achingly unfashionable in his drab brown suit with his grubby beige raincoat folded across his lap, had a kind of avuncular affection for the girl with her purple asymmetrical hair and her many studs and perforations.

'When we last spoke, Erin,' he said, 'you was working on some new software. How's that going?'

'Oh, my Remote Deletion programme . . . yes, going very well. I've tested it a few times and the results are very promising.'

'Sorry, you've lost me, dear,' said Mrs Pargeter. 'I'm afraid I'm rather clueless when it comes to computer stuff.'

'The programme I've been working on,' Erin explained, 'enables me to get into any other computer and delete any files I want to from it.'

'But don't people have lots of back-ups these days?' objected Truffler. 'External hard drives and memory sticks and clouds and things . . .?' His words ran out. That was the full extent of his IT knowledge.

'Yes, but the genius thing about this programme I've invented,' said Erin, 'is that it can recognize where copies of the documents have been stored – and wipe those too!'

'Blimey,' said Truffler. 'How does that work then?'

'If I started explaining you'd be here all day. Probably most of tomorrow as well.'

'And still probably not understand it.' Mrs Pargeter smiled. 'Anyway, your new programme isn't what we're here to talk about, is it, Erin?'

'No.' The girl went into efficient businesswoman mode. 'Well now, are either of you active on social media?'

'What, you mean that Facebook and Twitter nonsense?' said Mrs Pargeter. 'Good heavens, no. I don't want people sending me photographs of their lunch.'

'I use Facebook a bit for getting information,' Truffler admitted reluctantly (he was unwilling to reveal any short-coming in his anti-technology stance), 'but I don't use it for my social life.'

'Why not?'

'Because I don't have a social life.' This was said without any tinge of self-pity. Truffler Mason was a workaholic. There was genuinely nothing that he enjoyed more than pursuing his investigations – particularly when that involved working with Mrs Pargeter.

'Well, I'd be lost without my social media,' said Erin.

'It's a generational thing,' said Mrs Pargeter. 'I've always preferred meeting people face to face. Then you can tell what they're thinking as well as what they're saying.'

Erin grinned. 'Which is one of the reasons I invited you to come here rather than talking on the phone or emailing.'

'Good.'

'Anyway,' Erin went on, 'I use Facebook and Twitter a lot. Like you say, Truffler, very useful for finding out certain kinds of information. But there's another online social networking service I use a lot more.'

'I haven't heard of any others apart from Facebook and Twitter,' said Mrs Pargeter.

'Oh, there are quite a few lesser-known ones. The one I'm talking about's relatively new – and it's directed at a very specific clientele.'

'Oh? Who's that then?'

'Well, you've heard of people being "detained at Her Majesty's pleasure" . . .?'

'Yes,' said Mrs Pargeter cautiously. 'I've heard of them. Never met any, of course.'

'No, Erin wasn't suggesting you might have done,' said Truffler hastily – and diplomatically.

'A lot of good friendships are built up by people in those

circumstances,' the girl went on. 'And when they . . . er, return to lives where they have more freedom . . . well, they like to keep in touch.'

'Oh yes,' said Truffler. 'There's a magazine for them, isn't there? Called *Inside/Out*. Lets people know who's being released when, that kind of stuff. Very useful – particularly if people are putting a team together for a big job, they like to know people's availability. Handy for the wives and girlfriends too. Gives them a bit of warning to get their latest blokes off the scene before hubby comes home.'

Mrs Pargeter listened to this with a look of innocent incomprehension in her violet eyes, but she made no comment.

'You're dead right, Truffler,' Erin continued. 'In fact it's the *Inside/Out* people behind this new social network. You know, a lot of magazines these days are ceasing to have print editions and just going online.'

'Yeah. So, is the online version still called *Inside/Out*?'

'No, they've got a much better name for it.'

'What's that then?'

'ClinkedIn.'

'Oh, very good, yes.'

'Anyway, as I say, I find ClinkedIn incredibly useful for a lot of the research work that I do. It's a very good way of contacting individuals who, er, might have reasons of their own why they don't want to be contacted. A lot of the people who register do so under pseudonyms for . . . well, also for reasons of their own. And you'd be surprised how readily some blokes will grass their mates up when they know it's being done pseudonymously.'

Again Mrs Pargeter's face showed mild incomprehension.

'But,' Erin went on, warming to her theme, 'suddenly in the last few days I've noticed a new clue being laid down.'

'Sorry?'

'Oh, I should have explained, Mrs Pargeter. It's ClinkedIn jargon. When you start a new topic, it's called "laying down a clue", and all of the messages linked to that clue are kept together in the same "strongbox". That's another technical ClinkedIn term. It is, incidentally, a virtual strongbox, not a real one. But, anyway . . . it's going to be simpler if I show you this on the screen.'

The laptop was instantly flipped open and Erin's deft fingers on the keys immediately found what she was looking for. 'That's the first clue that was laid.'

She turned the laptop round so that her two guests could see the screen. At the top was the ClinkedIn logo of two hands joined at the wrists by a pair of handcuffs. Then below was the message, the 'clue' that had been 'laid'.

It read: 'Will anyone who has any information about the career of Mr Pargeter, who used to operate in the Essex and East London areas, please contact me through the usual ClinkedIn method.'

His widow turned pale. 'I don't like this,' she said.

Her eyes travelled down the screen to the name of the person who had laid the clue. 'Snowy'. 'Mean anything to you, Truffler?'

He shook his long head. She looked at Erin Jarvis.

'No,' the girl replied to the unspoken question. 'I've been through all the records. Nobody who worked for your late husband ever used the nickname "Snowy".'

'Doesn't ring a bell with me either,' said Mrs Pargeter. 'I haven't seen it in the little black book he left me.'

'I think it's something that clue-layer has made up just to post this.' Erin's finger pointed at the screen.

Mrs Pargeter looked disturbed. Mr Pargeter had always managed his affairs with great discretion. He had even trained up Public Relations officers to ensure that his name never attracted any kind of publicity. It pained her to think how unwelcome this kind of intrusion would have been to a man whose life had been devoted to avoiding ostentation of any kind. If there was one thing Mr Pargeter had always hated, it was being the centre of attention.

'The question is,' said Truffler, 'whether that message has prompted any replies.'

Erin thrust her lower jaw out ruefully, as she moved round the table and reached between them to use the keyboard. A couple of flicks of her fingers produced a screen full of messages. 'Seems like a lot of people have memories of your late husband.'

This observation did not make Mrs Pargeter look any happier. 'Any of the names mean anything to you, Erin?'

'No, again I've checked them and all of them seem to be using nicknames made up specially for the occasion.'

Truffler Mason had been studying the screen intently. 'And none of them do actually give any information, do they? Just, like, offer to set up meetings with Snowy, and that's when presumably they would spill the beans.'

'That's quite common on ClinkedIn,' said Erin. 'A lot of the type of people who use it have a strong aversion to putting anything in writing.'

'Just like your husband always recommended, Mrs P,' said Truffler.

But for once a remark like that didn't elicit any fond reminiscence. Mrs Pargeter looked distinctly ruffled.

'Are there more of these messages – clues?' Truffler asked.

Erin scrolled down with her hand and produced another screenful. 'Again, no names I could recognize.'

'Well, you're not going to find any names you recognize, are you?' said Truffler. 'No one who was genuinely close to Mr Pargeter would have volunteered this kind of information. We all knew what he was like, how careful he was about security. That first clue from Snowy was effectively asking blokes to grass him up, and none of us who ever worked for him would dream of doing that. The only people who're going to offer that kind of info are people who'd been his rivals, people who'd worked for the other side. *Criminals*,' he concluded with distaste.

He was watching as Erin continued to scroll through an ever-increasing series of messages. Something caught his eye. 'Just a minute – stop there!'

She did as instructed. Truffler pointed out a long finger. 'Well, there's a name I recognize. No attempt to disguise that one.'

They all read the words. '"Wirecutters" Wilson'. Mrs Pargeter and Erin Jarvis looked at him blankly. The name meant nothing to them.

Truffler's voice was even more doom-laden than usual as he said, 'Do you remember Streatham?'

Only the one word was required. They both knew immediately what he was talking about. 'Streatham' was one of the very few major jobs which had ended in failure for the late Mr Pargeter. And it had failed because some of his most trusted associates had betrayed him. Mrs Pargeter, who of course had never known any details of what was planned or what went wrong, still always blanched when she heard the word 'Streatham'.

'But surely that was all sorted out,' she said. 'Julian Embridge was the traitor on that occasion and he is detained at Her Majesty's pleasure for a good few more years yet.'

'Yes, Julian Embridge was the mastermind,' Truffler agreed, 'but there was others involved too. Among them . . . was "Wirecutters" Wilson.'

'I don't like this,' she said for the second time.

And she meant it.

TWELVE

The following morning Mrs Pargeter had another call from Rochelle Brighouse. 'I thought it was probably time for me to tell you what I want from you.'

'I agree. I've never been a believer in beating about the bush.'

'Nor have I.'

'You said it wasn't money, Rochelle.'

'Oh no, it's not money. One can always find money, but there are other things that are more exclusive and more valuable.'

'You also said you'd have documentary evidence to back up your claim.'

'Yes, I did, didn't I? Well, I don't think we need bother about that.'

'Really? It's possible my lawyers might feel differently.'

'Melita, I'm sure you don't really want to introduce lawyers into this.'

'Oh? And why not?'

'Because it's the kind of thing that can be more effectively sorted out on a one-to-one basis. We're both intelligent women.

We're related by marriage. I'm sure we can come to some kind of accommodation about this.'

The frostiness remained in Mrs Pargeter's voice as she responded, 'I would say that rather depended on what "this" is.'

'It's something that my brother left to you and to which I believe I have a right.'

'And what is that?'

'It's the little black book in which he recorded all the names of the persons with whom he worked.' There was a silence. 'I'm not asking for the actual book. You can keep that. I just want a photocopy of the contents.' Again no response. 'You do know what I'm talking about, don't you, Melita?'

'I know exactly what you are talking about, Rochelle.'

'And your reaction is?'

'My reaction is that my husband left his little black book to me, and I am not about to give it away to anyone else. Even his sister. Do I make myself clear?'

'You may think you make yourself clear, Melita, but I don't believe you have thought through the consequences of what you are saying.'

'Oh? And what might those consequences be?'

'The last time we spoke, Melita . . .' Mrs Pargeter didn't like the constant repetition of her first name. She also knew that Rochelle Brighouse knew she didn't like it, and therefore resisted saying anything on the matter. '. . . I mentioned that there were lots of secrets in Epping Forest.'

'Yes.'

'And then, only a few days later, Doreen Grange's body is found there.'

'Are you threatening me, Rochelle?'

'Oh, I wouldn't call it threatening. Just making you aware that . . . there is a bigger picture.'

'Well, it's a picture in which I do not wish to feature.'

'You speak as if you have any choice in the matter, Melita.'

And with that enigmatic observation, Rochelle Brighouse rang off.

Leaving Mrs Pargeter feeling somewhat uneasy. It was the fact that Rochelle knew of the existence of the little black book that troubled her. It made her wonder how much else she might know about the activities of the late Mr Pargeter.

She rang Truffler and reported the conversation she'd just had.

He sounded alarmed. 'Do you think you're in immediate danger? If you are, I'll drop everything and come out to Chigwell to protect you.'

'That's very sweet of you, Truffler, but entirely unnecessary. Rochelle was just making idle threats – nothing to worry about.'

'If you're sure . . .' He sounded very dubious. Like Gary, if he ever detected the mildest threat to Mrs Pargeter, he was programmed to leap instantly to her defence.

'Absolutely sure,' she replied firmly. 'Now are you getting anywhere tracking down those ClinkedIn people?'

'That's what Erin and I are doing right now. I'm over at her place. As you know, she's the whizz with all this online stuff.'

'Of course.'

'No names yet, but she thinks she's on a very promising track and hoping to find some results soon.'

'These are the people who responded to the original clue?'

'That's right.'

'And dare I ask if you're getting anywhere on the identity of "Snowy"?'

Truffler sounded more doleful than ever as he replied, 'That may be more difficult.'

'Oh well. Give Erin my love and wish her luck.'

'Will do.'

'And anything new on the Doreen Grange murder?'

'Not much yet. I've been in touch with Bobby the Bill. Only new information he's got is that they may have identified the drug with which she was sedated before being strangled.'

'What was it?'

'New one to me. Called butorphanol.'

'I've never heard of it either. Any more detail, Truffler?'

'Yes. Apparently it's a drug that's very rarely used on humans . . .'

'Oh?'

'. . . but it's in common use to anaesthetize animals before surgery.'

'So vets use it?'

'Very definitely.'

'Hm.'

'Anyway, Bobby the Bill says they're waiting for the full postmortem report. Should have it in a couple of days.'

'And then he'll pass the contents on to us?'

''Course he will, Mrs P. But are you sure you're going to be all right?' he added anxiously.

'I'll be fine.'

She felt warmly reassured by Truffler Mason's concern. Of course she'd never replace the feeling of security she had enjoyed while her husband was alive, but he had organized a very efficient protective team to look after her in his absence.

Although that thought comforted her, she still felt a level of frustration. Doreen Grange had been murdered and Mrs Pargeter felt she should be more proactive in solving the crime. But she couldn't think what her next step in that process should be.

Since she got the report from Truffler about Jasmine Angold's dire financial straits, Mrs Pargeter hadn't had time to take any action to alleviate her friend's situation. She had organized similar philanthropic help for other of her late husband's associates, and she knew that her approach must be tactful and oblique. She was dealing with proud and upright people who would not wish to feel that they were the beneficiaries of charity.

As a result, with the help of Truffler Mason, Mrs Pargeter had devised a variety of ways to explain to people the sudden influx of money into their bank accounts. The discovery of a fictitious insurance policy taken out by a prudent husband had satisfied many widows. An inheritance from an unknown – and indeed non-existent – relative had also worked very well. And the unearthing of a stash of cash in Epping Forest (London's go-to destination for such windfalls) never failed to convince.

Mrs Pargeter was just assessing which of these methods of improving Jasmine Angold's financial situation would be most apposite, when the object of her charity rang her. As ever unsurprised by such synchronicity, she greeted her friend warmly.

Jasmine was ringing, it soon became clear, because she had only just heard the news of Doreen Grange's death. 'Isn't it terrible?' she said. 'A harmless old lady like that. And we only met her a few days ago. And she crocheted those lovely little cats, didn't she? I'll treasure mine even more now, knowing that it was probably one of the last ones she ever made. You didn't buy one, did you?'

'No, I didn't.'

'Bad luck. I bet you're regretting it now, aren't you?'

Mrs Pargeter let that pass without comment, as Jasmine went on, 'Actually, it wasn't only about Doreen Grange that I was ringing.'

'Oh?' Maybe Jasmine was going to talk about her finances. That would give a perfect cue for Mrs Pargeter to take action.

But no, the woman was too proud to do that. Instead, she said, 'I've been thinking a lot about Edna.'

'Oh?' At that moment Mrs Pargeter couldn't for the life of her think who Edna might be.

Fortunately, Jasmine elucidated. 'You know, my cat. The one who died in January.'

'Oh yes. Yes, of course.'

'Well, I think I am ready to get a replacement for her. Obviously it'll never be the same with a different cat, but I dare say in time I could learn to love her.'

'Got to be a her, has it?'

'Oh yes. Toms can be tricky. Spraying all over the furniture, that kind of thing.'

Mrs Pargeter, who knew little of feline behaviour, took Jasmine's word for that.

'And I really think the best place to look for a new cat would be PhiliPussies.'

Mrs Pargeter greeted this idea with enthusiasm. She needed a reason to find out more about Mendy Farstairs' charity, and Jasmine Angold was providing it on a plate.

'And I wondered . . .' Jasmine hesitated, '. . . because I'm still not very confident . . . you know, since Silver died . . .

about going to places on my own . . . I wondered if you'd mind coming with me . . .?'

Mrs Pargeter couldn't have asked for a more attractive or timely invitation.

THIRTEEN

G ary picked up Mrs Pargeter from Chigwell in the Lexus, then drove to Romford to get Jasmine Angold, who wasn't quite ready when they arrived. The chauffeur waited while Mrs Pargeter went inside. Jasmine introduced her daughter Charley, saying, 'She'll get you a cup of coffee if you like. Just got to finish my make-up. I daren't be seen out without the full warpaint these days.' Then she rushed upstairs.

Charley Angold had her mother's sharp features, but her colouring was all from her father. Mrs Pargeter had never met 'Silver' Angold, but there were enough family photographs around the sitting room to show him to have been a rosy-cheeked man with almost Nordic blond hair and piercing blue eyes. These characteristics he had bequeathed to his daughter.

Charley had risen on Mrs Pargeter's arrival from the laptop on which she had been working. 'Would you like some coffee?'

'No, thanks, love. Had some just before I went out.' She gestured towards the computer. 'Can I ask what you're working on?'

Charley grimaced wryly. 'Trying to write a book.'

'Oh? What kind of book? A novel?'

'Yes, I suppose so.'

'You don't sound too sure.'

'No, I'm not.' Mrs Pargeter waited. She could always tell when someone had more confidences to share. And sure enough the girl went on, 'It's something I sort of promised my dad.'

'Oh?' Mrs Pargeter knew only the smallest of prompts would be required.

'Yes, he was very keen on my writing.'

'Really?'

'At school I always did well at English. Dad was very proud of that. I mean, as someone who'd never had much education himself, he did value academic achievement . . . perhaps more than it should be valued.'

'Oh?'

'I wrote some stories in my teens and he just loved them,' said that one day I'd have a book published.'

'And that hasn't happened yet?'

'No, I'm not sure that it ever will. You see, in spite of his lack of education, my dad loved the English language. He had great respect for people who could use it brilliantly. Loved words, Dad did. He taught himself how to do crosswords when he was inside for . . .' She corrected herself '. . . when he had a period of enforced leisure. Quite tricky crosswords he did, used to sometimes finish *The Times*. He tried to get me interested in them, but I couldn't see the point. I mean, I tried to understand the attraction of it, but it just seemed like playing with words. I think my brain's differently wired from the way Dad's was.'

'But you were very close to him?'

The girl nodded. Even after more than a year, her eyes glistened at the memory. 'Yeah, I'd do anything for Dad. I'm an only child and, well, there's always a strong bond between fathers and daughters. My first memories are of being with him. He used to take me on walks and make up stories for me. There was one particular walk we'd do in Epping Forest. Took me there when I was tiny in my buggy, and the last time we went it was the other way round, me pushing him in a wheelchair, only about a week before he passed.' She brushed away a tear forming on her eyelid. 'He called that walk "The Fairy Path", and he always told me stories about fairies when we went along there. There was a "Fairy Ring" where he said they danced through the night.' She sniffed forcibly to break her mood. 'Oh well, he's gone,' she said flatly.

Mrs Pargeter was intrigued. 'And you say he wanted you to write a book?'

'Yeah. Like his dying wish. Left a letter for me, sealed up, to be read after his death.'

Mrs Pargeter still couldn't get her head around the strange request. 'And the letter said that you should write a book?'

'Yes. You can see it if you like.' Charley gestured to a much-handled envelope on the table. 'I keep it here and when I get really stuck on the writing – which is quite often – I have another look at the letter to convince myself that Dad really wanted me to write the bloody thing.'

'It's awfully nosy of me, but do you mind if I read the letter?'

Charley Angold handed the envelope across. 'Be my guest. Maybe you can see some let-out in it for me, so that I don't have to pretend to be a writer.'

The letter which Mrs Pargeter extracted was as much handled as its envelope. And this is what she read:

Dear Charley,
Might your old father give you a word of advice?
Might your old father point you in a useful direction?
Ask who always loved you from when you were a tiny
   baby?
The champion who stood up for you against everyone?
Only me.
You stirred in me emotions I did not know I had.
I did not expect to feel such total love,
Such a subtle change in my personality
From a rough, uncaring man to a helpless father,
Hopelessly enthralled by this perfect person
Whose tiny life had suddenly become so important to me.
So know my love is there forever,
Whether I live a reasonably long time or die young.
But there's a last thing I want you to do for me,
Do not think me terrible to ask this . . .
But I always felt pleased when you did well at English.
So, for me, your old Dad, please write a book,
Get it published, into major bookstores
And other outlets, even e-books if you must,
So long as it is out there existing for the general public
   to read,
You will know for sure that you have done the right thing
   by your poor old Dad
And I will be able to rest easy wherever it is I end up.
What kind of book you write . . . it doesn't matter to me,

So long as the thing is published in some form or other,
Be it hardback, paperback or presentation copy.
I know you may find it's hard but, if you ever loved me,
Do as this letter tells you and lo – all your wishes for
    future prosperity
For you and for your mother should instantly come true.
Follow my instructions – into your writing
Go line by line and progress letter by letter
Until you at last attain the moment of publication.
Then my vast fortune will be yours – and Jasmine
Will benefit too from that vast, vast fortune.
My blessings always will support you both.

When she finished reading, she saw that Charley was looking at her expectantly. 'Well, you see anything in there that says I don't have to write a book?'

Mrs Pargeter shook her head wryly. 'Sorry, I don't. It's a strange letter, though.'

'I agree. Strange thing for any father to ask his daughter to do. I mean, it'd be different if I'd ever expressed any interest in writing a book.'

'That wasn't why I said it was strange.'

'Oh?'

'I mean, it's laid out in a strange way. And the language is quite sophisticated.'

'For an uneducated crook, are you saying?'

Ice frosted over Mrs Pargeter's violet eyes. 'No, Charley, that is certainly not what I'm saying.' But the *froideur* only lasted a moment. 'It's laid out more like a poem than a letter. Don't you find that odd?'

The girl shrugged. 'Not really. My dad educated himself. As I say, he loved language and while he was ins—' She saw a warning look and made the correction '. . . when my father found he had time on his hands, he read a lot. He had a big vocabulary, but I don't think he ever got round to learning rules of grammar or how writing should be laid out properly. He would have loved to have written a book himself. Maybe that's why he's inflicted this wretched task on to me.'

'Do you really have to do it, Charley? I know you loved your father very much and would have wanted to please him, but you do have your own free will. Would it be so terrible if you were to give up the book and go back to your job?'

The girl grimaced. 'Trouble is, Mum's now got rather obsessed by it.'

'By the idea of you having a book published?'

'Yes. She keeps saying it's something that I've got to do in my father's memory.'

'Oh dear.'

'You're right. It is a bit of a bind. I had a perfectly good job in retail. Ladies' dress shop, you know. I loved it, but Mum said I really ought to give it up and concentrate on my writing. Which is daft, because it means I'm not contributing anything to the family finances, which are always pretty rocky. Income was erratic enough when Dad was alive, but now Mum's on her own . . .' Charley blushed. 'I shouldn't be telling you all this. Mum's very proud about things to do with money.'

'Don't you worry about a thing,' Mrs Pargeter soothed. Already plans were forming in her head about ways of alleviating Jasmine Angold's financial insecurity. If a publisher could be found for Charley's book, then perhaps the advance paid could be augmented by the Pargeter millions . . . It was a thought . . .

But not a thought that could be pursued at that moment, because Jasmine, warpainted up to her most exacting standards, had just appeared in the doorway.

The English end of the PhiliPussies operation, Bailey Dalrymple's clinic in Leigh-on-Sea, was very smart. But then the residents of Leigh-on-Sea reckoned everything there was smart; certainly a cut above anything to be found in its rather raffish neighbour, Southend-on-Sea.

The clinic was probably a converted house, Mrs Pargeter guessed, with four or five bedrooms. Though they stayed on the ground floor, sounds from upstairs suggested that the whole space was used for veterinary purposes rather than as residential accommodation.

Bailey Dalrymple was as beamingly bonhomous as he had been at the PhiliPussies reception. Mrs Pargeter, who had rung to make the appointment, and Jasmine Angold had been ushered into his office by a young woman in a nurse-like green uniform. The reception area could have been that of a five-star hotel, the only giveaways to its real function being the proliferation of dog leads, cat collars and other pet impedimenta hanging from the walls behind the welcome desk. And Bailey Dalrymple's domain, with its panelled walls and brown leather chairs, could have been a private room in a gentleman's club. His tweed jacket, striped tie and burgundy corduroys reinforced the image.

It was clear that PhiliPussies was a high-end operation. Mendy Farstairs subsidized it a great deal, Mrs Pargeter surmised, but she could also see why the fundraising services of Rochelle Brighouse might also be required.

'So . . .' said the vet, when they had done the introductions and been supplied with coffee, 'you're after a cat, Mrs Pargeter?'

'No, no, sorry. I booked the appointment, but in fact it's Jasmine who wants a cat.'

'Oh, apologies for the confusion. Well, Mrs Angold, you've certainly come to the right place. We have a wide variety of cats for you to choose from.'

'And are they . . . you know . . .' Jasmine asked tentatively, 'I mean, considering the fact that they've come from Greece, where they may have just been wandering around without a proper owner . . . are they house-trained?'

'They certainly are, Mrs Angold. True, a lot of them aren't when they arrive here. And some of them are quite wild, almost feral. But it's our policy here at PhiliPussies not to give the cats to new owners until they've spent a couple of months here doing all those necessary things – learning to use the litter tray, being neutered, microchipped and so on.'

'And do you have any kittens?'

'Ah, Mrs Angold. No, I'm afraid we don't. Or very rarely. It sometimes happens that one of the cats is expecting when she arrives here. But usually termination is part of the neutering process. So I'm afraid what you'll be getting here is a mature cat. And of course we can't be precise about the age, but if you've been dealing with cats for as long as I have, you can make a pretty good guess at it.'

'I see. That sounds fine.' If Jasmine had really had her heart set on a kitten, she was hiding her disappointment very well.

'So, given the fact that you can have virtually anything so long as it's not a kitten, do you have any specific requirements in the cat you get?'

'Well, it would be a replacement for a much-loved pussy who died of old age in January.'

'I'm very sorry to hear that,' said Bailey Dalrymple, with the professional solicitude that Mrs Pargeter felt sure he used when he had to put down someone's precious pet. 'And what was your cat's name?'

'Edna.'

'Ah. A female, I take it?'

'Yes. And I think I would like another female. I know they'd be neutered, but I've never really taken to toms.'

'No worries, Mrs Angold. I have almost equal numbers of males and females.'

'Oh, good.'

'Any other specifications?'

'Well, I don't know . . . I'm never going to replace Edna, so I'm not sure whether to go for a cat that will remind me of her or plump for something completely different which won't raise memories and comparisons.'

'And what colouring was Edna?'

'She was tortoiseshell. Beautiful tortoiseshell.'

'Ah. Well, of course it is completely your decision, Mrs Angold, but I do have a particularly beautiful tortoiseshell cat who's about two years old and with whom I think you might immediately fall in love.'

Excitement sparkled in Jasmine's eyes. 'Ooh, can I see her?'

'Of course. If you'd both like to follow me . . .'

Bailey Dalrymple's prediction was correct. Jasmine Angold did fall instantly in love with the tortoiseshell he showed her. Though on some of them the ginger can be very ginger and the black and white very black and white, on this cat the markings were muted, pale, almost as if they had been painted in watercolours rather than oils.

She was thin, like the other Greek cats on display, but would no doubt soon be fattened up by an indulgent British owner. Some of the cats were in cages – 'those are the most recent arrivals,' Bailey Dalrymple said, 'not quite civilized yet' – but most seemed to have the freedom of the house's large back garden. It was walled in wire netting and roofed in the same material, so that not even the most determined and devious of cats could escape.

Though there was a certain amount of mewling and the occasional mock-battle going on, the residents of the garden seemed mostly placid and well behaved. The cages were spotlessly clean and no smell emanated from the rows of litter trays. Two girls dressed in the same green uniforms as the one who'd let the visitors in wandered among their charges, tending to their various needs.

The tortoiseshell endeared herself to Jasmine by coming straight up and coiling her slender body around the potential owner's legs. She submitted happily to being picked up. An experienced cat-lover, Jasmine tickled the creature under its chin and then ruffled the loose skin on the back of its neck.

As she did so, her finger caught on something. She looked closer and saw that a thin line of the fur had been shaved and three or four stitches closed over a wound. 'What happened? Was she in a fight with another cat?'

'No,' the vet replied. 'That's where she's been microchipped.'

'But surely a microchip is tiny. Only about the size of a grain of rice. It doesn't need a cut like that to install it.'

Bailey Dalrymple grimaced. 'I agree. And if I were microchipping a cat I'd inject the thing and not leave a mark. Sadly, the Greek vets seem to be rather clumsier than I am. With a lot of the cats that arrive I have to do a bit of remedial surgery – sometimes even replace the microchip. But don't worry about it, Mrs Angold. That scar'll have cleared up in a few days.'

'Oh, I know it will.' As she continued to be stroked, the cat began purring like a road drill. She knew which side her bread was buttered, and recognized in Jasmine a devoted owner who would be obedient to her tiniest feline whim.

'I must think of a good name for her.' The decision that she was going to keep the cat had required no thought at all. 'Something Greek . . .'

Mrs Pargeter's knowledge of classical Greek literature was limited, but she thought she would probably recognize the name of whichever goddess Jasmine selected. She was therefore a little surprised when her friend said, 'Nana.'

'Nana?'

'After Nana Mouskouri. She's Greek.'

'Oh yes, of course she is,' said Mrs Pargeter.

Jasmine Angold turned to Bailey Dalrymple. 'Will I be able to take Nana with me straight away?'

'There shouldn't be any problem with that. She's had all her injections, got her new microchip. No, she's good to go. All we need to do is sort out the payment. If you'd like to come back to my office . . .'

Mrs Pargeter hadn't really considered whether the cat would have to be paid for. PhiliPussies was a charity, after all, but perhaps charging for its Greek rescue cats was another one of its fundraising initiatives. She caught Jasmine's eye. Clearly her friend hadn't thought much about payment either.

'How much you pay,' Bailey Dalrymple said when once again ensconced in his club-like milieu, 'depends really on the individual. Obviously it's hard to put a price on a living creature like a cat.'

'It's not that hard,' objected Mrs Pargeter. 'If it's a rare breed like a Burmese or a Siamese, then you'd expect to pay a premium. But when you're just talking about a stray moggy who's been rescued from outside some Greek taverna, well . . .'

'But PhiliPussies is a charity,' the vet countered. 'And the people who take the cats from us generally recognize that and are accordingly generous.'

'How generous?' asked Mrs Pargeter, who was beginning to find Bailey Dalrymple's unctuousness a little wearing.

'There's usually a minimum donation of two hundred and fifty pounds. Some people obviously give more.'

She looked at Jasmine Angold. If Mrs Pargeter didn't already have information about her friend's parlous financial situation, the expression on her face spelled out that she couldn't readily access two hundred and fifty pounds.

Instantly Mrs Pargeter's hand was in her handbag, then proffering a credit card to the vet. 'Put it on this . . .' Jasmine was about to object, but her friend went on firmly, 'And you can settle up with me later.'

Bailey Dalrymple whipped a payment machine out of a desk drawer, inserted the card and asked, 'Now how much would you like it to be, Mrs Pargeter?'

'You said two hundred and fifty was the minimum . . .?'

'Well, it's not set in stone. It's entirely according to what the purchaser wishes to give, but usually people start at two hundred and fifty.' He could smell the money on Mrs Pargeter. 'Though those who can afford it have been known to be considerably more generous.'

'Oh well,' she said, 'if it's not set in stone, and if it's entirely according to what the purchaser wishes to give, take a hundred off my card.' Though Mrs Pargeter was the most generous of women, if there was one thing she didn't like, it was being ripped off.

With very bad grace, Bailey Dalrymple entered the figure quoted and passed the machine back for Mrs Pargeter to enter her PIN. Jasmine Angold looked deeply embarrassed, but at the same time comforted by the ease with which Nana had taken up residence on her lap, as if it had been her haven of choice for many years.

Mrs Pargeter, needless to say, felt no such qualm of embarrassment. And as she took the receipt that was handed to her, she reckoned it was time to take up the investigative opportunity that their visit to PhiliPussies offered.

'Very sad about Doreen Grange,' she observed.

'Oh, you heard about that?' said Bailey Dalrymple, mildly surprised.

'It would be hard not to hear about it. The story has been all over the news media for days.'

'Yes,' he agreed. 'I just wasn't aware that you knew of the connection between her and PhiliPussies.'

'We met her at the Baronet Hotel reception.'

'Ah.'

'I bought one of her lovely little crocheted cats,' Jasmine interpolated.

'Oh. I'm afraid I didn't see you on that occasion.' He looked at his watch. 'Well, now we've sorted out the cat for you Mrs Angold, I do have rather a busy morning ahead of me and I'm afraid I—'

Ignoring his words, Mrs Pargeter pressed on, 'One would have thought Doreen Grange was the last person to get murdered. It's difficult to imagine her being involved with criminals.'

'I wouldn't have thought she was involved with criminals. Her death was more likely just one of those sad events which happen in life. She was just in the wrong place at the wrong time. Mistaken identity, perhaps. Or she surprised an opportunistic burglar who didn't want to be identified by any witnesses.'

'No, it couldn't be that. Doreen was staying with her sister Flora in Rayleigh. And there was no sign that the house had been broken into. She appears to have left in the middle of the night of her own accord.'

'Really?' said Bailey Dalrymple peevishly. He hadn't anticipated that Mrs Pargeter would know so much detail about the case. 'Well, look, I'm sorry, but as I say I do have a lot of work to—'

But Mrs Pargeter steamrollered through. 'Is Doreen's loss going to have a big effect on your work here at PhiliPussies?'

'Won't make much difference. We can always find another cat-besotted old biddy to . . .' He seemed to realize that this was not the most appropriate of responses. 'That is to say, everyone involved in the charity deeply regrets Doreen Grange's death. She played an invaluable role in the operation of PhiliPussies, and her contribution will be sorely missed. But I am sure that, in time, we will find a suitable replacement.'

'Yes, I'm sure you will.'

'And now, if you could—'

But Mrs Pargeter wasn't finished yet. 'So who do you think might have killed Doreen Grange?'

'I have absolutely no idea. I know nothing about the details of the case, apart from what I have seen in the television reports. Nor, in fact, did I know Doreen Grange very well. I had only met her on a couple of social occasions – you know, PhiliPussies functions like the event in Billericay.'

'But nobody,' Mrs Pargeter insisted, 'hears about the murder of someone they know – however vaguely – without having some thoughts about who might have done it. It's human nature.'

'It may be your human nature, Mrs Pargeter, but I'm afraid mine does not involve itself in such ghoulish conjectures.'

'Oh, go on, you must have thought of someone.'

Perhaps realizing that offering her the name of a suspect was the only way he was going to get Mrs Pargeter out of his office, and out of his hair, he conceded a suggestion. 'The motive for the majority of murders is something domestic. Within the family. Husbands killing wives, wives killing abusive husbands, worms turning, that sort of thing. Well, we know Doreen never married, but she does seem to have been utterly loathed by her sister. If I were a police detective involved in this investigation, the first thing I would do is set up a very thorough investigation of Flora Grange.'

After Bailey Dalrymple's office door had closed on him, Jasmine was persuaded by the green-clad girl on reception to buy a very expensive cat transporter for Nana. While she made the purchase, Mrs Pargeter noticed that, amid the wide variety of dog leads on show, a good few were tartan. Interesting.

FOURTEEN

Mrs Pargeter was thoughtful after Gary had dropped Jasmine off in Romford and continued to the mansion in Chigwell. She had a lot to think about.

And she didn't really reckon she'd got much useful information out of Bailey Dalrymple. For him to shift the suspicion for Doreen Grange's murder on to her sister was an obvious ploy. The fact that the two didn't get on was well known, but they both seemed to have come to terms with the antipathy. When two people have become used to mutual hatred – as in many marriages – it takes some sudden change of circumstances for that situation to turn to violence. If the status quo is survivable, it becomes endurable. Aspirations, on both sides, are lowered accordingly.

And Mrs Pargeter couldn't think what change of circumstances between Doreen and Flora Grange might have led the younger sister suddenly to top the older. She recalled that Flora had implied she was a victim of blackmail by Doreen, but that again sounded like a state of affairs that had been established for a very long time.

No, she didn't seem to be getting anywhere in her investigation into the murder of Doreen Grange.

The other thing that continued to perturb her was the arrival in her life of Rochelle Brighouse and her sister-in-law's interest in the little black book. Most frustrating of all, Mrs Pargeter was convinced there was some connection between the two annoyances, though she couldn't for the life of her think what it might be.

It was not in Mrs Pargeter's nature to blame anyone other than herself for her lack of progress. Truffler Mason and Erin Jarvis, she knew, were busy trying to search out the identity of the 'Snowy' who had laid the clue on ClinkedIn. They were also checking out the people who had responded to the request for information about the late Mr Pargeter. These people were, by definition, Mrs Pargeter's enemies. Nobody loyal to her husband would have dreamed of revealing any information about him.

Not for the first time since his death, she wished he was there beside her. He had always been such a practical man, so good at soothing away anxieties. Mr Pargeter had always been a solutions man; whatever problem threatened, he was always confident he could find a solution to it. And he always did.

But Mrs Pargeter knew there was no point in getting maudlin. She had had the best years of her life with her husband, but now he was dead she had to make the best of what was left to her. She too was a pragmatist.

Given that her husband wasn't there, her next natural recourse was to his invaluable bequest to her. The little black book could help her out, as it had so often in the past. Its listings might include some undiscovered expert, whose skillset would match perfectly the requirements of her current problem.

The portrait of her in the sitting room was hinged on the left-hand side so that it opened like a window to reveal the complexities of the safe door behind. There were rows of keypads, knobs and flashing LED lights, familiar to Mrs Pargeter but impenetrable to any potential thief.

She flicked her way through the well-remembered sequence of codes until finally a small metal shutter slid up to give access to the screen behind. In a practised way Mrs Pargeter pressed her thumb against the glass.

Instantly the safe door opened.

All her jewellery, the gold ingots and the neat stacks of banknotes were exactly where they had been when she'd last accessed the interior.

But of the little black book there was no sign.

FIFTEEN

Parvez the Peterman's dark face was as near as it could get to ashen as Mrs Pargeter once again moved back the portrait and opened the safe. 'I feel so humiliated,' he said. 'When I think of all your husband did for me, and I am not even capable of keeping his wife's valuables secure.'

She shrugged. She wasn't denying the disastrous significance of the theft, but it was not in her nature to apportion blame. 'I suppose for every technological advance you make in your business, there's a whole bunch of criminals trying to work a way to get through it.'

'Of course they are doing that. I should know. I was one of them. When I worked with Mr Pargeter, I was always trying to get one jump ahead of the villains in the other gangs . . .' Something he saw in her violet eyes caused his words to dwindle into silence.

'When you installed this safe, Peter, you said there was only one person in the world who was in with a chance of cracking it.'

'Right. "Tumblers" Tate.'

'But you said he was dead.'

'Yes.' Parvez the Peterman didn't sound as certain as he had the first time he'd made the assertion.

'You really don't think there's anyone else?'

He shook his head wryly. 'No one with Tumblers' level of sophistication, no. Oh, there are a lot of bright young kids coming out of university with their technology degrees who think that the fact they've got some letters after their names means they can get straight in at the top of the tree, but to be a proper cracksman you need to have served a long, hard apprenticeship – exactly as I did with your late husband. When I think how useless I was when I started out – I could hardly get through the simplest Chubb lock, but he was very patient. He stuck by me, ignored my early mistakes and gradually put me on to bigger and bigger jobs. I remember there was a bank vault in Neasden where . . .'

Once again, something he saw in Mrs Pargeter's eyes deterred him from proceeding further with his reminiscences.

'So you still believe the only person who could have got into this safe was Tumblers Tate?'

'Yes, I'd definitely say so.' There was awe in his voice. Clearly Tumblers Tate, despite working for the opposition, had been an idol for Parvez, someone by whose standards all of his own achievements must be measured and always come up short.

'Though,' Mrs Pargeter suggested, 'his being dead might have made the job a little trickier.'

'You're right there.' Parvez the Peterman rubbed his stubbled chin thoughtfully.

'Are you sure he is dead?'

'Well, I assume he must be. Old Anno Domini suggests that, apart from anything else. I mean, he always seemed as old as the Dead Sea Scrolls when your husband was up against him and the rest of the Lambeth Walkers. I was younger then, of course, and maybe I'd thought he was older than he was, but I'd say he had a good twenty years on me – and I'm well into my sixties now. Hm, I wish there was some way of finding out whether a villain's dead or not . . .'

'Do you know,' said Mrs Pargeter, 'I think there might be.'

Erin Jarvis answered the phone on its first ring. 'Mrs Pargeter,' she said, informed by her mobile screen who the caller was. 'How lovely to hear from you.'

'Nice to talk to you too, Erin.'

'I wish I had more to report on the identity of "Snowy" and the others prepared to talk about working with your husband, but I'm afraid—'

'Don't worry about that. I'm sure you'll get there. No, I was actually ringing about something else . . . something I thought you might be able to find out through ClinkedIn.'

'Tell me what it is, Mrs Pargeter, and I'll make every effort to get you an answer.'

'I knew you would, Erin. Well, listen . . .' She filled the girl in on everything Parvez the Peterman had told her about Tumblers Tate. 'And all we really want to know is: Can he possibly still be alive? And if he is, where can we find him?'

'Leave it with me, Mrs Pargeter. I'll lay a ClinkedIn clue straight away and see what it turns up in the strongbox.'

'Good girl, Erin.'

It never occurred to Mrs Pargeter that the theft of the little black book could be the work of anyone other than Rochelle Brighouse. She didn't think her recently discovered sister-in-law had actually broken into the Chigwell mansion and cracked the safe herself, but she felt sure that the actual perpetrator – Tumblers Tate or whoever – was acting on Rochelle Brighouse's orders.

She rang the mobile number she had stored on her phone. There was no reply and she was not offered the option of leaving a message.

So she went online and googled 'Rochelle Brighouse Public

Relations'. Everything she knew about the woman suggested that she would use her own name as her brand identifier.

She rang the number and asked to speak to the boss. A very well-spoken girl at the other end of the line told her that Rochelle Brighouse was on a week's holiday. Might it help if the caller were to speak to her personal assistant?

'No, no worries,' said Mrs Pargeter. 'I'll give her a bell next week. So where's she gone to . . . somewhere nice?'

The well-spoken voice replied, 'Greece. An island called Atmos.'

Though Rochelle Brighouse had her mobile firmly off, Mrs Pargeter wondered whether there might be another way of contacting her through Mendy Farstairs. The two women clearly knew each other well. But when she rang the number of the Farstairs' (no doubt enormous) pile, the phone was answered by a woman with a thick Eastern European accent who identified herself as 'the housekeeper'. She regretted that Mrs Farstairs was away. When asked where her employer was, the woman replied, 'Greece. She's at her place on Atmos.'

But she did give Mendy's mobile number which, while the mood was on her, Mrs Pargeter rang.

It was answered immediately, even eagerly, as if Mendy Farstairs had been expecting a call. She sounded marginally disappointed when Mrs Pargeter identified herself.

'Oh, how nice to hear from you.' Mendy seemed puzzled as to why she was being called.

'I just wanted to say,' Mrs Pargeter improvised wildly, 'that I and a friend visited the PhiliPussies clinic in Leigh-on-Sea recently and—' she lied – 'we were very impressed by it.'

'Good.' Mendy Farstairs's tone was warmed by the flattery. 'Bailey Dalrymple does a wonderful job there.'

'My friend did actually buy a cat. She's delighted with it.'

'Oh, that's so encouraging to hear. It makes everything we do seem worthwhile.'

Mrs Pargeter's improvisation became more focused – and her lying more extravagant. 'And, you know, since I came to that reception at the Baronet Hotel, I've been wondering whether I should make some kind of donation to PhiliPussies.'

'Anything is always welcome.'

'Yes, I'm sure.' Mrs Pargeter went into helpless-little-woman mode. 'It's terribly difficult when one has a lot of money to decide where one should give it. There are so many charities around, so many conflicting claims on one's attention and resources.'

'I agree. But I always think one has to check very carefully how a charity is run. There are a lot of charlatans out there.'

'You're so right, Mendy.'

'And of course I make sure that PhiliPussies is run according to the strictest possible moral principles.'

'I'm sure you do.'

'So,' Mendy went on, moving into fund-raising mode, 'were you to make a donation to us, you would know that you were dealing with a bona fide charity, whose operations would stand up to any scrutiny.'

'Mm. I was planning,' Mrs Pargeter lied on, 'to have a holiday soon, island-hopping in Greece . . .'

'I'm sure you'll enjoy it. The weather out here is absolutely gorgeous.'

'. . . and I was wondering, if it turned out that my tour took me to Atmos . . .'

'You'd be most welcome any time,' said Mendy keenly. 'Then you could inspect the Greek end of our business, which I'm sure you will find is just as well run as the Leigh-on-Sea operation.'

'Thank you. Well, if I am likely to come to Atmos, I'll let you know.'

'Splendid. And, now you've rung me, I've got your mobile number.'

'Of course.' Though Mrs Pargeter had the latest iPhone, she very rarely used it for anything other than making calls. Texting seemed to her more trouble than it was worth.

'Thank you so much,' said Mendy. 'And remember, if you do come, Mrs Pargeter, there's always a spare bed for you here at Villa Rufus.'

'Got quite a lot of info very quickly,' Erin announced. 'Lot of people on ClinkedIn used to have connections with the Lambeth Walkers and "Knuckles" Norton.'

'Sorry? Who?'

'Knuckles Norton was the boss of the Lambeth Walkers.'

'Ah.' Mrs Pargeter did not give any indication that she'd heard the name of the gang before as Erin went on, 'And a lot of them knew about Tumblers Tate – by reputation at least.'

'But is he still alive?'

'Remarkably, it seems that he is, yes. Well into his nineties, I gather, and claims to have retired a long time ago . . . though one or two of the replies suggested he might still take on the occasional "special job".'

Mrs Pargeter felt pretty sure that the theft of her little black book from Chigwell would probably qualify as a 'special job'. A special job contracted to Tumblers Tate by Rochelle Brighouse. She was angry at the thought of what her sister-in-law had done, upset by the thought of some stranger breaking into the precious security of her Chigwell mansion, and she wanted revenge. 'So where can we find him?' she asked. 'Some shooshed-up South Coast retirement home?'

'No,' Erin replied. 'He retired abroad.'

Mrs Pargeter knew the answer before she had to ask the question.

And sure enough, Erin said, 'Greece. An island called Atmos.'

'Truffler,' she said when she got through to the Mason de Vere Detective Agency, 'how d'you fancy a trip to Greece?'

SIXTEEN

Hamish Ramon Henriques, known universally as 'HRH', still had his office in Berkeley Square. Only a small brass plaque by the panelled door, which read 'HRH Travel', gave an indication of the vast business empire he ran from the address.

Gary always knew what car was appropriate to each situation and, visiting a building opposite Jack Barclay, London's premier Bentley dealership, obviously required him to drive the same marque. He parked firmly on the double yellow lines outside the HRH offices and, after he had helped Mrs Pargeter and Truffler Mason out, used his old trick of placing a Metropolitan Police Commissioner's cap on the back window shelf. Since first using the ploy, he had never received a ticket.

When Mrs Pargeter announced her name through the entry grille, the door was opened immediately by a perfectly groomed, grey-uniformed receptionist, who had the name 'Karen' on her gold badge. After fulsomely welcoming her guests, she pressed a button on her console and an equally well-groomed girl with 'Farron' on her badge appeared to escort the visitors to the lift. On the first floor they were greeted at the lift's doors by another immaculately presented girl badged 'Saffron', who led them through an aisle between rows of grey-suited beauties busy on their phones. As they passed, Mrs Pargeter and Truffler heard snatches of their public-school-voiced conversations.

'. . . don't worry, the uranium itself will be put in a lead-lined shoe-polish tin which you can carry in your hold luggage and which will not be detected by any of the scanners . . .'

'. . . and of course when the airbag inflates it is guaranteed to asphyxiate anyone sitting in the front passenger seat. No need to thank me, sir, that's all part of the HRH service . . .'

'. . . which means the name on your passport will be "Pastor Willikin van der Beer", and your forwarding address will be The Church of the Immaculate Revelation, Santiago. Yes, sir, quite a change from Wormwood Scrubs, I agree . . .'

'. . . then, once you get to the clubhouse, all you have to do is dismantle the Number Five iron and reassemble it into an assault rifle which has slightly more firepower than the Kalashnikov AK-47. How you use it, of course, is up to you . . .'

As she heard these snippets, the level of innocence in Mrs Pargeter's violet eyes did not alter one iota. They were focused on the open office door at the end of the aisle, in which stood the benign figure of Hamish Ramon Henriques, his arms opened wide in greeting.

Though it was a few years since Mrs Pargeter had last seen

him, the specialist travel agent had not changed at all. The flow of his white hair and the droop of his white moustache still instantly brought to mind images of Don Quixote. His black eyes sparkled either side of his high-ridged nose. And, despite his exotic Iberian appearance, he still dressed in the heavy tweeds of a British gentleman.

His voice too was redolent of public schools, clubs in St James's and Lord's Cricket Ground. 'Mrs Pargeter,' he rumbled, as he enveloped her in his arms, 'it is such an enormous pleasure to see you!'

'You too, HRH. You remember Truffler?'

'Of course. How could I forget? When I think of the number of times he and I worked together with your late husband, which was always an enormous pleasure for both of us. I remember with particular relish the getaway hovercrafts which I organized after the raid on the Thamesside offices of . . .' At a look from Mrs Pargeter, his words petered away to nothing. 'Anyway,' he resumed, 'please come through into my office and let me know how the devil I can help you. If you'd like tea or coffee, Saffron will of course organize that for you.'

Mrs Pargeter asked for an Americano with hot milk on the side; Truffler wanted 'an ordinary coffee – white, two sugars.'

'Now, Mrs Pargeter,' said HRH, once they were all ensconced in generous leather chairs in his office, 'what can I do for you?' He spread his hands wide. 'As you know, for you I'll do anything. When I think about how your late husband helped me, nurtured my career . . .' A discreet cough from Mrs Pargeter, who sometimes heard almost too much of this kind of gratitude, did not stem the travel agent's effusion of good-will. 'Change of identity, new passport, arranging travel to a destination which has no extradition treaty with the UK . . . just tell me what you need and I will supply it.'

'Well, it's not as complicated as all that stuff,' said Mrs Pargeter. 'I just want you to arrange transport for me and Truffler to go to Greece.'

'Greece again, eh? I seem to remember that's what I was asked to fix for you last time we had dealings. Is it back to Corfu?'

'No. This time it's an island called Atmos.'

'Not one I've heard of.'

'I believe it's quite small.'

'Nearest island with an airport is Skiathos,' said Truffler, who had done some research.

'Oh, fine. Anyway, it'll be no problem. I'll get someone to take the details.' HRH pressed a button on his desk. The door opened immediately and another grey-clad paragon appeared. 'Lauren, could you take the details of Mrs Pargeter's travel requirements and sort it out, please?'

'Of course, HRH. First class, I assume?'

'Oh, that'd be nice,' said Mrs Pargeter.

'No, no, forget scheduled flights,' said the travel agent. 'We'll do this with one of Barry's private jets.'

'And what then – the ferry from Skiathos to—?'

'Good heavens, no, Lauren. It is Mrs Pargeter we're dealing with here, not some odorous student backpacker. Get Apostolos to organize one of his speedboats to take her the last leg to Atmos.'

'Very well, HRH.'

'So, Mrs Pargeter, if you'd just tell Lauren your requirements . . .'

These were quickly given. The flight, it transpired, could be arranged for later that afternoon, but Mrs Pargeter, thinking of the packing she needed to do, opted for eleven o'clock from London City Airport the following morning.

Mrs Pargeter had quickly decided not to take up Mendy Farstairs' offer of a bed at Villa Rufus. The owner's presence might inhibit her investigative activities. So she asked about accommodation, and Lauren instantly had the information at her fingertips. Atmos, it turned out, though it had a lot of fairly primitive beds available in private houses, only boasted two hotels. One, according to Lauren's research, was just a few rooms above a taverna, rather scruffy and noisy in the evenings. The other, the five-star Hotel Thalassa, was much more Mrs Pargeter's style. She and Truffler were quickly booked in there for an open-ended stay beginning the next day.

Once the arrangements had been made, Mrs Pargeter reminded herself that, as a long-term associate, HRH might know something of her late husband's sister. She had encountered uncharacteristic reticence on the subject from Truffler and Gary, and wondered whether HRH might be a little more forthcoming.

But no, his initial reaction was equally curt. Yes, he did know that the late Mr Pargeter had had a sister. But no, he knew nothing about Rochelle Brighouse.

'She runs a company called "Rochelle Brighouse Public Relations".'

'Doesn't mean anything to me.'

'And I have reason to believe that she has stolen the little black book which my husband left me.'

That did finally make an impression on HRH. Like all of Mr Pargeter's former associates, he knew the inestimable value of the little black book. 'Is this why you're going to Atmos, Mrs Pargeter?'

'One of the reasons.'

For a moment he stroked his trailing moustache thoughtfully. Then he said, 'I have not met Rochelle Brighouse, but I have had dealings with her son.'

'Haydon?'

'Yes. He had somehow got my name and came to my office, asking me to arrange a trip for him.'

'Where to?'

'Costa Rica. He claimed that he had just done a major bank job in London and needed to lie low for a while.'

'I'm not entirely sure what you're talking about,' said Mrs Pargeter innocently, 'but did you make the arrangements for him?'

'No. I didn't believe him. I knew he was lying.'

'How?'

'Because I can always make a list of the complete personnel behind any bank robberies committed in London, and Haydon Brighouse certainly wasn't involved in any of the recent ones.'

Here was one of the many occasions in her life when Mrs Pargeter refrained from asking any further questions. Where HRH got his information from was entirely his own business, and definitely not an area into which she would wish to probe.

'So why did he come to see you and start telling lies?'

'I can only think that he was trying to find out information

about my company and how it works. Haydon Brighouse is a
journalist of some kind. I know for a fact that he has written
books about criminal gangs like the Krays and the Richardsons.'

'Ah.' Mrs Pargeter had forgotten being told that particular
piece of information at the PhiliPussies reception. 'You're
right.'

'Also, there was a very odd thing that happened after Haydon
Brighouse left my office.'

'Oh?'

The travel agent picked up a fountain pen from his table.
It was classically styled, black with gold bands and a golden
pocket clip. 'I'm a bit of a connoisseur when it comes to pens.
I feel if my signature on a document is valuable – which it
most certainly is – then the instrument with which I write that
signature should also be valuable. It's a little snobbery of mine,
if you like.'

'Doesn't sound like there's any harm in it,' Mrs Pargeter
reassured.

'My view entirely. This one I'm holding is in fact a
Montblanc Meisterstück Red Gold Fountain Pen. They cost
a lot of money . . .'

'I'm sure they do.'

'. . . though I always think it's rather vulgar to be too specific
about the precise cost of things.'

'I couldn't agree with you more, HRH.'

'Anyway, I have a collection of these pens, but what happened
after Haydon Brighouse had left this office that day was that
the one that had been on my desk during our conversation . . .
was no longer there.'

'You think he'd nicked it?'

The massive shoulders shrugged. 'What else is there to
think, Mrs Pargeter?'

She was thoughtful. She remembered the disappearance of
the gold cat necklace at the Baronet Hotel reception. Haydon
Brighouse had been very near the display when all the lights
went out. Could there be a connection between the two thefts?
But for the time being she kept her thoughts to herself.

'Strange, though,' HRH mused. 'I'm absolutely certain no
one on my team would have taken it – there's not a drop of

criminal blood in any one of them. Same with the cleaning staff – all vetted to the highest level of security. I suppose the pen could have just been dropped, fallen into a wastepaper basket and thrown away, but that seems unlikely. No, I think young Master Brighouse must've taken it.'

'Are you going to go after him and try to get it back?'

'Oh, good heavens, no. As I say, I do have quite a collection of them. No, I just thought it was odd behaviour, a so-called journalist coming here and nicking stuff.'

'Hm. And you think his main purpose was to get information about your operation and how everything works?'

'I think so, yes. Not that I'm really worried about the guttersnipes of the Press,' said HRH. 'I have a very efficient legal department who would instantly stop at source any insinuations or adverse publicity about the legality of my business, but if there's one thing I don't like, it's a snooper.'

'Oh, I couldn't agree with you more,' said Mrs Pargeter.

The unpleasant moment, the thought of an outsider trying to infiltrate his perfectly run operation, had passed. Hamish Ramon Henriques beamed at his visitors.

'Now,' he said, looking at his watch, 'lunch at the Connaught, don't you think?'

SEVENTEEN

The hotel was built on the ruins of an old monastery, looking down over the tiny harbour of Atmos. The little bay was a naturally sheltered semicircle, with one curve extended by the stone-built harbour wall, against which an assortment of local fishing vessels and luxury yachts were moored. On the other arm a row of rocks, resembling the ridged back of some ancient dinosaur, sloped down into the sea. In one of the rocks the motion of the water had hollowed out a narrow archway, through which small boats could pass into the open waters of the Aegean. Though it seemed inconceivable on a still summer's day, violent storms would sometimes batter the little island of Atmos and, because of the number of fishing boats which had failed to negotiate the rocky archway, it was known locally as 'The Widowmaker'.

Mrs Pargeter had not known until the darkly moustached owner of the hotel pointed out the view from her suite that 'Thalassa' was the Greek word for sea, but now she saw how appropriate the name was. The Mediterranean was a perfect deep blue, broken only by the white crests of wavelets as they approached the rocky shore.

'Thank you, Vasilis,' she said.

'And Mr Mason's room is right next door.' He gestured as he spoke. 'This door here leads to it. The door can be locked or left open, according to your wishes.'

Mrs Pargeter smiled inwardly at the implication of his words. Though she loved Truffler Mason dearly, the idea that they might have any physical relationship would have been as incongruous to him as it was to her. Still, hotel owners like Vasilis had to be ready for all eventualities.

So all she said was, 'Thank you, I'm sure I'll be very comfortable here.'

But whether she would be successful in her investigations was, of course, another matter.

'Spoilt for choice, aren't we?' said Truffler. They were sitting on a vine-shielded terrace at the front of the Hotel Thalassa. The private investigator, for whom the idea of a holiday was totally alien, did not appear to possess any leisurewear. He still wore his perpetual light brown suit and a tie was tightly knotted around his neck. Over the back of the chair next to him was his inevitable beige raincoat. To Truffler's mind, although it seemed hot enough at that moment, you never knew what horrors the weather might be storing up for you.

He was sipping a Mythos beer, Mrs Pargeter a very acceptable local white wine. Both glasses sparkled with icy condensation.

'How d'you mean?' she asked in response to his question.

'Well, as to where we start investigating. Do we go after Tumblers Tate first? Or Rochelle Brighouse?'

'Well, I think we ought—'

She was interrupted by her mobile ringing.

'Hello?'

'Welcome to Atmos!'

The voice was unmistakable. 'Oh, thank you so much, Mendy.'

Mrs Pargeter didn't ask how the woman knew of their arrival on the island. She got the feeling that there were few secrets on Atmos.

'I was wondering whether you'd like to come over to Villa Rufus for a drink . . .?'

'Well, that sounds a very nice idea.'

'When you like. I see you're having a drink on the Hotel Thalassa terrace right now.'

'What?' Though Mendy's knowledge of their arrival had not caused any anxiety, her most recent words had given Mrs Pargeter the uneasy feeling of being under surveillance.

The woman seemed able to read her mind. 'Don't worry, I'm not spying on you. It's just that Villa Rufus is right next to the hotel. I'm the terracotta-coloured building just to your left.'

Mrs Pargeter looked in the direction indicated. The adjacent estate was only separated from Hotel Thalassa by a low stone wall. And in front of a splendidly renovated villa stood Mendy Farstairs talking on her mobile phone. She wore a pale blue linen shirt over baggy white linen trousers, and waved when she saw Mrs Pargeter looking at her.

'Why don't you and your friend come over straight away?'

Mrs Pargeter agreed that they would, ended the call and quickly brought Truffler up to speed with what was happening. Then she grinned and said, 'When you asked whether we should go after Tumblers Tate or Rochelle Brighouse, I was about to say that our first port of call should be Villa Rufus. And that's where we're going.'

There had been no stinting with Rufus Farstairs' money in the conversion of his wife's villa. ('His wife's' was how he regarded it; he had no interest in spending time there. Generously, he never begrudged any expense which kept Mendy quiet and, preferably, out of the country.)

Villa Rufus was built on another part of the monastery ruins on which the Hotel Thalassa had been constructed. It was a large, two-storey house with, Mrs Pargeter estimated, at least six upstairs bedrooms. On the swirl of gravel in front of the empty garages stood a Range Rover and an open-topped BMW sports car. The interior of the house, through which Mendy Farstairs led them, was deliciously air-conditioned, and contained more ancient Greek statuary than the average Athens museum.

At the back of the villa, sparkling in the Mediterranean sun, was a half-Olympic-size swimming pool. The heavy air of the vine-covered terrace was stirred by invisible fans. Mendy sat her guests down on richly padded loungers, and then turned to a moustached man in a white jacket and black trousers who stood behind a drinks trolley. 'Now Yannis will get you a drink. What would you like?'

They opted for more of what they had been drinking at the hotel.

'You are happy at Thalassa, I hope,' said the man called Yannis. He must have seen some surprise in Mrs Pargeter's expression because he said, 'Of course we knew you were coming here. Vasilis who runs the hotel is my cousin. So is Apostolos who brought you here in his speedboat.'

Mrs Pargeter realized that the man who'd so expertly skippered her from Skiathos had exactly the same moustache as Vasilis and Yannis. Small wonder that there appeared to be no secrets on Atmos.

'They're all cousins here,' Mendy confirmed. 'All members of the Philippoussis family.'

'Like Costas, the one who runs this end of your charity?'

'Exactly. And do just tell me when you want to see the cats' sanctuary we have here.'

'Yes, of course.' Mrs Pargeter had to remind herself that the stated aim of her visit to Atmos, so far as Mendy Farstairs was concerned, was to assess whether PhiliPussies was a charity worthy of the investment of some of her millions. 'Is it nearby?'

Mendy gestured towards the end of the garden, where a colonnade of pillars, perhaps looted from some temple, marked the boundary. 'Just through there. I'll show you whenever you like.'

'Well, maybe when we've finished our drinks . . .?'

'Fine. As you like.'

There was a silence. They sipped contentedly. Then Truffler Mason, who wasn't a natural at making small talk, said, 'Lovely place you've got here, Mrs Farstairs.'

'Oh, please call me Mendy.' Their hostess clearly couldn't place Truffler, couldn't quite work out why he was accompanying Mrs Pargeter. Maybe, like Vasilis, she too thought they might be an item. The very idea made it hard for Mrs Pargeter to suppress a giggle.

'Well, Mendy . . .' Truffler continued his heavy-handed social progress, '. . . is there quite a big expatriate community out here?'

'On Atmos? Good heavens, no. It's a tiny island, one which I'm glad to say mass tourism has yet to discover. I mean, the total population is under three hundred.'

'And almost all of them have the surname Philippoussis,' Yannis contributed.

'And all have moustaches?' Mrs Pargeter suggested slyly.

'Yes.' He erupted with laughter. 'Especially the women!'

This unwelcome sexist banter was not what Mrs Pargeter had been hoping to stimulate but, having worked out the direction in which Truffler's questions were tending, she asked, 'So are there any other Brits on the island?'

'A couple of other villas have English owners,' Mendy Farstairs replied dismissively, 'but they're never here. They're not part of the Atmos community,' she concluded with the very definite implication that she, by contrast, was part of that community. Pressing the point home, she added, 'Whereas I am virtually an honorary Philippoussis.'

Yannis chuckled dutifully. This was clearly a line she wheeled out with some regularity.

Truffler persisted. 'So there are actually no other permanent British residents on the island?'

'No,' said Mendy, then recalled something to mind. 'Well, there is an elderly gentleman who lives in an old fisherman's cottage down by the sea, but from all accounts he's virtually a recluse. Bedridden, I gather. Touch of dementia too, I've heard. I've never met him.'

Truffler Mason hid the little spurt of excitement that her words prompted in him. 'Does he live on his own?'

'There's a woman called Theodosia who looks after him. I don't think she lives in.'

'Theodosia Philippoussis . . .?' suggested Mrs Pargeter.

Yannis let out a loud laugh as Mendy confirmed the woman's surname.

'Whereabouts is this place where he lives?' asked Truffler casually.

'You go down to the harbour, then walk along the shoreline to the right. The house is virtually on the beach. Painted white, needless to say. Red tiled roof.'

Truffler nodded, taking in the information, and exchanged a covert look with Mrs Pargeter. She knew exactly what he was thinking.

So she was unsurprised when, after refusing a top-up drink and saying she'd like to take up the offer of touring the cat sanctuary, Truffler Mason said he wouldn't come with them. Picking up his raincoat, he announced that he fancied stretching his legs 'with a stroll down to the harbour.'

EIGHTEEN

Mendy Farstairs led Mrs Pargeter along the side of her perfect blue swimming pool, through the displays of ancient Greek statuary towards the cat sanctuary. Overelaborate wrought-iron gates were open at the front. As they passed, Mrs Pargeter noticed a large chain and padlock hanging from one of them. Apparently the place needed tight security.

The buildings which housed the Greek end of the PhiliPussies operation were of the same high spec as the clinic in Leigh-on-Sea, but less welcoming. There was no reception area, no cosy office for the entertainment of visitors. But then presumably there were very few visitors to the facility. It was only at the English end that potential owners came to inspect the goods on offer.

As a result, the complex of buildings looked more like a military institution than anything else. The individual units were brick-built, but all had metal doors which could be closed with latches and padlocks.

The behaviour of the sanctuary's inmates was also markedly different from those in Leigh-on-Sea. The Greek cats that had been given sanctuary by Mendy Farstairs were distinctly ungrateful for her magnanimous gesture. They had enjoyed their semi-feral life round Atmos harbour, basking in the shade beneath parked cars, darting out and weaving around the wooden legs of rush-seated taverna chairs, scavenging the food dropped (either accidentally or deliberately) by tourists, wolfing down the guts and entrails left by the fishermen on the harbour walls. They had relished the nights of caterwauling and fierce quick casual sex. Incarceration in cages – of however high a spec – was far from being their idea of fun.

So the noise of feline complaint, which grew in volume as Mendy Farstairs and Mrs Pargeter approached the sanctuary, was fairly overpowering.

So was the smile and bolted-on charm of Costas Philippoussis. His lips below the obligatory dark moustache were thin and the brown eyes flickered with cunning. He was all over Mrs Pargeter.

'Of course I have been expecting you. I hope Apostolos Philippoussis, who is my—'

'Cousin?' Mrs Pargeter hazarded.

'Yes. I hope he give you a good journey from Skiathos.'

'Very pleasant, thank you.'

'And I hope you have been made welcome at Hotel Thalassa by Vasilis, who, as it happens, is also—'

'Your cousin?'

'Yes. But please, let me show you around the sanctuary here. I gather you are perhaps maybe considering making an investment in the PhiliPussies charity.'

'Perhaps maybe,' Mrs Pargeter echoed.

Mendy Farstairs let Costas do most of the talking during

their guided tour. He was very efficient, but Mrs Pargeter got the impression that he was also quite prickly. The slightest murmur of criticism riled him. He was proud of the way he did his job and resented any disparagement of his skills.

For example, when Mrs Pargeter asked if he had any veterinary training, Costas immediately became very defensive. 'Of course I do. I have degrees, diplomas.'

It wasn't her habit to grill people, but something in the man's manner made her distrust him. So she asked, 'Degrees and diplomas in what?'

'Well, obviously. Veterinary qualifications.' Then he backtracked a little, which made Mrs Pargeter absolutely certain he was lying. 'The educational system here in Greece is a little different to what you have in the UK, but my degrees and diplomas have their equivalents in your country.'

From this Mrs Pargeter concluded he had no relevant qualifications at all. So he'd pulled the wool over Mendy Farstairs's eyes on that subject. In how many other ways, she wondered, had Costas deceived his employer? The founder of PhiliPussies made no secret of her considerable wealth – indeed the construction of Villa Rufus and the cat sanctuary trumpeted it abroad – so she would be the perfect innocent mark for the kind of conman Mrs Pargeter increasingly, even on such short acquaintance, recognized Costas Philippoussis to be. Still, it was not the moment to challenge him. She must maintain her role of potential investor.

The sanctuary complex contained a surgery, full of shining metal surfaces and featuring what to Mrs Pargeter's uninformed eye looked like a state-of-the-art range of veterinary equipment. There was a gleaming stainless-steel table in the centre of the room, which somehow had to be the place where any actually surgical procedures happened. Remembering Bailey Dalrymple's strictures on the quality of Greek microchipping, she rather tentatively brought the subject up.

'So is this where you would do the microchipping of the cats?'

'Of course.' Was Mrs Pargeter being hypersensitive to detect a new caution in Costas Philippoussis's manner? He went on,

'It is very important that we keep a track of these animals, in case they get lost.'

'Or escape back down to the harbour where they came from?' she suggested.

'Yes, but that very rarely happens. Our security here is very tight.'

Mrs Pargeter looked through the window to the serried ranks of cages full of yowling cats and could not help but agree.

'And do you do the microchipping yourself?' she asked, mindful of Bailey Dalrymple's reference to Greek 'clumsiness'.

'Of course. There are other helpers here, but—'

'All cousins?'

'Yes, all cousins,' he replied without humour, 'but I am the only one who has the qualifications to do surgery on the cats.'

'I see. And do you actually have to do surgery?' Mrs Pargeter persisted.

'Of course I do. Some of the cats have accidents, they get into fights. Some are brought in with broken limbs. For them surgery is essential.'

'No, what I actually meant was – do you have to do surgery when you microchip the cats?'

'Yes.'

'But I thought a microchip was a tiny—'

'Mrs Pargeter, the state of veterinary practice is constantly changing. New techniques are being invented all the time, particularly in the area of microchipping.'

'But surely—'

'Mrs Pargeter,' Costas Philippoussis almost bellowed, 'with the greatest respect, I don't think it's appropriate for you to question me about professional issues of which you have no understanding!'

Why is it, she thought wryly, that when people start a sentence 'with the greatest respect', they always go on to demonstrate no respect at all?

The instructions to the white cottage on the beach had been very clear, and Truffler Mason soon found himself in front of its faded and paint-blistered once-blue front door. He knocked and was quickly confronted by a generously proportioned woman in a black dress with a black apron tied round her substantial middle. Truffler knew that in Greece her garments probably denoted widowed status.

'You must be Theodosia Philippoussis,' he surmised. And yes, Yannis had been right – she did have a moustache.

'Theodosia Philippoussis, *vai*,' she responded.

'My name is Truffler Mason. I'm a friend of Mr Tate's.' It was somewhat stretching the meaning of the word 'friend', but allowable in the circumstances.

The blankness of Theodosia's expression suggested he could stretch whatever English words he wanted to and she still wouldn't understand any of them.

Truffler placed his two large hands on his chest and tried the old British trick of speaking more loudly. 'Me – friend – Mr Tate.'

The blankness remained blank.

Truffler had another go. 'Mr – Tate,' he said very slowly and loudly.

That got through. Theodosia nodded and repeated the words. 'Mr – Tate.'

Truffler gestured to the interior of the house. 'Mr Tate – in here?'

But that was a linguistic step too far. She didn't understand him.

Truffler Mason wasn't getting anywhere, so he tried another approach. Reaching his wallet out of his back pocket, he produced a card with his photo on it. Very formally he showed this to Theodosia. 'Police,' he said, knowing that the word was identical in most languages.

That did impress her. Alarm replaced the blankness of her expression. 'Police – Mr Tate?' she asked.

Truffler nodded gravely as he returned the card to his wallet. No need for her to know that she had just been shown an out-of-date membership card for a gym which he had joined in a fitness frenzy some years before and only visited once.

Theodosia stood back to let him in. The front room was white-painted and bare of anything but the most basic furniture. After the heat on the beach it was very cool, insulated by the cottage's thick stone walls. She closed the front door, then raised her hands and pointed to a blue taverna chair with a woven rush seat, indicating that he should wait. She went through another door into the back.

There was an open laptop on the table next to him. Its screen was blank. Truffler touched a key and the machine came out of sleep mode. He looked at the images displayed, then must have jogged something because a new window opened. He looked at its contents in puzzlement until the screen once again darkened.

This was one of those rare occasions when Truffler Mason wished he knew a bit more about the new technology. Generally, he was quite content with his status as Luddite dinosaur, but from time to time more than a basic knowledge of computers might have proved useful. The first image he had seen on the cottage laptop had been self-explanatory. The second, to his eyes, had meant nothing.

And yet he felt sure it was something very simple which anyone who had a passing acquaintance with the ways of Windows would have recognized instantly. If only Erin was there with him on Atmos. Truffler thought of Erin a lot. His thoughts were in no way lascivious. 'Paternal' or 'avuncular' were more accurate adjectives. Perhaps for Truffler, Erin Jarvis was the daughter he never had.

He didn't dare touch the laptop again, in case he left signs of his curiosity. He looked at his watch, beginning to think he had been waiting long enough, wondering what might be delaying Theodosia, when she reappeared. She said 'Mr Tate' and circled a finger around the area of her temple in the international sign for mental fragility. Truffler nodded and rose to follow her.

The room he was led into was as simple as the first, again with the minimum of furniture. There was a bare wooden table with a couple more taverna chairs, and at one end an old kitchen range and rectangular stone sink. Theodosia stood back and gestured to the open doors which led to a yard at the back.

Truffler walked past her into the open air. The stone-floored space, backed by solid rock, was shaded by a roof of tilted bamboo so, though warmer than the interior, it was not as scorchingly hot as the beach.

The subdued light meant that his eyes took a moment to focus. Then he saw an ancient wooden-slatted white-painted lounger, on which lay an even more ancient man.

Tumblers Tate had aged a lot since Truffler Mason had last encountered him. That had not been a happy occasion. Normally the late Mr Pargeter's management skills had enabled him to avoid direct confrontations with business rivals, but every now and then he and his associates had been forced to meet their enemies face to face. That is what had happened some years before when a select group of the Lambeth Walkers had met Mr Pargeter's team one night when both had been attempting to withdraw cash from a branch of the Trustee Savings Bank in Neasden. Parvez the Peterman had been arranging entrance to the premises for Mr Pargeter, and Tumblers Tate had been doing the same job for his rivals. The result had been a lot of unpleasantness and a degree of violence. It was not an event that Truffler Mason looked back on with any enthusiasm.

To Truffler, all that time ago when he was in his late twenties, Tumblers Tate had already looked an old man, but now a stronger word than 'old' was needed. What lay on the lounger was a husk, a wisp of a human being. His parchment skin, mottled by exposure to the sun, looked stretched so thin that his bones might pierce through at any moment.

In spite of the humbleness of his surroundings, Tumblers Tate did not appear to be impoverished. He was dressed in smart blue linen trousers and a blue and white striped short-sleeved shirt. Round his scraggy neck hung a chunky gold necklace and both thin wrists sported matching bracelets. On the low table beside the lounger lay the latest iPhone, a brandy balloon and a bottle of Courvoisier Napoleon Cognac (which Truffler knew retailed at getting on for a hundred quid).

The faded watery-blue eyes were open, but showed no reaction to the new arrival, even when he said, 'Well, long time no see, Tumblers.'

From his great height, Truffler Mason looked down at the man who had been such a thorn in the side of the late

Mr Pargeter. On their team they had had the great skills of Parvez the Peterman, but even he admitted to being no challenge to Tumblers Tate. No lock could impede Tumblers' progress, no safe door keep out his prying hands. And, though his nickname dated from the days when he could align the key pins of any tumbler lock, as the security business became increasingly more electronic and sophisticated, he still managed to stay ahead of the game.

Like Parvez the Peterman, Truffler Mason did not believe that anyone else in the world could have worked through the layers of security installed in Mrs Pargeter's safe. And yet it seemed doubtful that the shrunken creature on the lounger could have moved as far as his kitchen, let alone made the long journey from Atmos to Chigwell.

Was there a new champion cracksman in the world, a successor, an apprentice to whom Tumblers Tate had passed on all of his expertise? It was an uncomfortable thought.

Truffler Mason was aware that, since she had ushered him into her employer's presence, Theodosia had been leaning against the kitchen doorway watching him. Though he felt confident that she genuinely could not understand English, he was still aware of her suspicion. He wondered for a moment whether her delay in letting him through to see Tumblers Tate had been caused by her telephoning someone – no doubt another member of the Philippoussis family – to announce his arrival at the cottage.

He had another try at getting a reaction from the old man. 'Come on, Tumblers, I know we wasn't always on the same side, what with you working for the Lambeth Walkers and all, but I'd've thought now we've reached a stage where we could let bygones be bygones.'

The watery eyes still gave no response.

Truffler chuckled. 'Funny, I often think back to the times when you and I was both – in our different ways – involved with the work of Mr Pargeter.'

Tumblers Tate had managed to betray no reaction so far, but hearing the name of his old adversary brought an involuntary twitch to his face.

Encouraged, Truffler went on, 'Ah, they was great times.

Of course, most of me old mates're going straight now. I'm a private investigator, you know, using much the same skills but, like, for a different purpose. Mr Pargeter was very good about sorting training and stuff for us, so that we could go into proper businesses after he had passed. What about your lot – they all turned legit too, have they?'

But, after his lapse on the mention of Mr Pargeter, Tumblers Tate was not about to give anything else away.

'Listen, Tumblers mate,' Truffler persevered, 'I know you can hear everything I say. I also know you can understand it, so can we drop the old dementia routine? It's not fooling anyone.'

The eyes flashed for a moment and focused a look of pure hatred on the visitor. Then Tumblers Tate spoke. His voice was reedy, but still demonstrated a surprisingly fierce vehemence. 'You give me one reason why I should say anything to you, Truffler.'

'Oh, I can think of a good few reasons,' said Truffler, pushing forward his advantage. 'For a start, you may think you're safe from the long arm of the law out here, Tumblers, but there's things I could pass on to the British police, certain bits of information which could make the rest of your life – however long or short that may be – very uncomfortable indeed.'

'Blackmail?' The old man spat the word out. 'That's never going to work. Because, you see, if you got dirt on me, I've got at least as much on you. I've kept a very detailed archive all of my professional life. So I could do exactly what you're proposing to do – and make your life equally uncomfortable.'

'Wouldn't work, Tumblers. One thing Mr Pargeter was always very good at was seeing all of his operatives ended up with clean sheets. You'd be amazed by the network of alibis he set up. Any job we done, everyone involved always could produce a witness to swear he wasn't near the scene of the crime at the time in question. All of us who worked for Mr Pargeter, we all supported each other on stuff like that.'

'Oh yeah?'

'Yeah.'

An evil smile played around the old man's lips. 'I think I could mention a few names of people who showed rather less solidarity with his associates.'

'Oh?'

'Let's say I mentioned the name "Julian Embridge" . . .?'

'Julian Embridge has been sent down for a very long sentence.'

'Maybe, but people don't become dumb when they're sent to the nick. Rather the contrary. A lot of them get very garrulous when they're asked to shop the people they used to work with. Besides, Julian Embridge wasn't the only one to leave the fold of Mr Pargeter's protection and work for the other side. The Lambeth Walkers ran a very efficient recruitment scheme.'

Truffler Mason decided that Tate's assertion was all too likely to be true, and abandoned thoughts of blackmail for a more direct approach. 'Listen, you know and I know that Mrs Pargeter's house in Chigwell was broken into and something very valuable was stolen from her safe there. You also know that you're the only cracksman in the world who could get through Parvez the Peterman's security to open that safe. So what I'm asking you is to own up to—'

Truffler became aware of sounds behind him. He turned to see Theodosia talking urgent Greek to Yannis, who had apparently just arrived. Seeing the visitor was facing him, Mendy Farstairs's factotum immediately stepped forward and said in insinuating English, 'I am sorry, Mr Mason, but Mr Tate is a very sick man. He cannot cope with the stress of visitors. As you see, he has lost the power of speech, as well as many other faculties.'

'He certainly has not lost the power of speech. He's just been talking to me as if—'

'Please, Mr Mason, I must ask you to leave.'

Tumblers Tate, grateful that rescue had arrived, slumped back on to his lounger, back to the torpor in which Truffler had found him.

Recognizing he was not going to get any more from that source, Truffler focused his interrogation on to Yannis instead. 'Listen, there's been a serious crime committed in England, a crime which only Mr Tate could have committed. I demand to know whether he has left the island of Atmos in the past few weeks.'

Yannis Philippoussis shrugged helplessly and gestured towards the wizened figure on the lounger. 'Leave Atmos? How could a man in that condition dream of doing such a thing? He cannot even go to the bathroom on his own. There is no way he could have travelled to England.'

Truffler was beginning to suspect that this might be true, so he tried another approach. 'But maybe he contacted someone in England and gave them instructions to—?'

'Mr Mason, I must ask you to leave. You are harassing a very sick man. If you persist in doing so, I will have to take further action. We do have a very efficient police force here on Atmos.'

'And no doubt they are all your cousins?' suggested Truffler.

'You are exactly right. They are,' said Yannis Philippoussis with a smug and unhelpful smile.

NINETEEN

'I wouldn't trust him further than I could throw him,' said Mrs Pargeter. She was referring to Costas Philippoussis, whose attractions for her had diminished with every minute he spent showing her round the cat sanctuary. 'I'm convinced he's cheating Mendy in a fairly major way, though I haven't yet worked out how.'

She and Truffler were seated at a table on the Hotel Thalassa terrace, as far away from the main building as possible, but still she spoke in a whisper. She had an increasingly uncomfortable feeling that there was a Philippoussis cousin listening behind every vine.

'Mendy has that gullibility of very rich people who've made no contribution to the accumulation of their money. Her husband Rufus is the one who's out there grafting away. If she'd had some part in making the money, she might be more careful with it. The trouble is that Mendy takes her wealth for granted, so it never occurs to her that people might be trying to help themselves to it.' Mrs Pargeter pursed her lips. 'It's very frustrating.' Then she grinned at Truffler. 'Still, I haven't asked you about your little excursion yet. Did you get anything out of Tumblers Tate?'

He grimaced. 'Not a lot.' And he recounted almost verbatim the conversation they had shared.

'So you don't think he's got dementia?'

'Far from it. He's as sharp as a tack, sharp as he ever was. Sharp as when he was back with the Lambeth Walkers.'

Not for the first time, the mention of this organization produced on Mrs Pargeter's face a look of innocent incomprehension.

'Anyway,' Truffler went on, 'I know for a fact that there's nothing wrong with Tumblers' mental faculties. All of the old boy's marbles are very firmly in place. There was a laptop in his cottage . . .'

'Oh yes?'

'. . . and when I touched it, it sort of came to life.'

'"Came out of sleep mode" is the expression that I think is used,' said Mrs Pargeter, who did not know a great deal about computers, but certainly more than Truffler did.

'OK, if you say so. Anyway, what was on the screen was *The Times* cryptic crossword. Today's – the date was there, and all.'

'Yes, I understand you can get most of the papers online these days.'

'Right. But the thing was . . . every one of the clues on that crossword had been filled in.'

'Ah.'

'Now Theodosia doesn't speak any English, so I can't see her getting far with *The Times* cryptic crossword, can you?'

'No,' Mrs Pargeter admitted.

'And I don't think Yannis or any of the rest of the Philippoussis cousins are going to make much headway on it either.'

Another, 'No.'

'So the only person in that place who could have solved today's cryptic crossword was Tumblers Tate himself. He's no more got dementia than I got the bubonic plague.'

'But did you check anything else on the laptop?'

'Didn't have time, really. And, as you know, I don't know

much about computers. But when I jogged the thing, another kind of picture come up. Quite bright blue, with instructions, I don't know what it was meant for.'

'Any writing? The name of the programme maybe?'

Truffler shrugged. 'There was some, but I can't remember what it said. Only saw like a glimpse of it.'

'Hm,' mused Mrs Pargeter.

Truffler let out a rueful chuckle. 'Where's Erin Jarvis when you need her, eh?'

Mrs Pargeter's mobile rang. Accustomed to the ways of synchronicity, she was totally unsurprised to hear that the call was from Erin Jarvis.

'We've identified the name of the person who laid the clue,' the girl announced excitedly.

'Sorry? Not quite sure what you mean,' said Mrs Pargeter. 'Maybe the Greek sun is fuddling my brain.'

'I'm talking about ClinkedIn.'

'Oh, of course. You're talking about the person who started making enquiries about my husband's business activities? "Snowy".'

'"Snowy", yes.'

'So who is he?' Mrs Pargeter asked excitedly. 'Will I recognize the name?'

'I'm afraid you will,' said Erin in a rather doom-laden way. '"Snowy" is Haydon Brighouse.'

'Ah.' Mrs Pargeter didn't ask how Erin had found out the information. She knew there was no point in questioning geniuses about their methods. 'So . . . what do you think he's up to?' She had an extremely accurate personal assessment of what he was up to, but she felt that this was one of those moments when a little tactical ignorance might fit the bill.

Erin spelled it out for her. 'As I'm sure you know, Haydon Brighouse, so-called journalist, is the author of books on the Krays and the Richardsons. I've also discovered that, under the "Snowy" pseudonym, he's been fishing for information on ClinkedIn about the "Lambeth Walkers", a gang led by a guy called Knuckles Norton, who were operating round the same time and on the same patch as your husband. So it seems he's planning a book on that rivalry, and any dirt he can get on Mr Pargeter will—'

'But he won't get any dirt on Mr Pargeter,' said Mrs Pargeter, her violet eyes at their most innocent.

'Why not?'

'Because there is no dirt to be got on Mr Pargeter.'

This statement was made in such a definitive manner that Erin Jarvis could only respond with a less-than-convinced: 'Right.'

'Still,' Mrs Pargeter mused, 'it's very important that Haydon Brighouse should be stopped from publishing any lies, isn't it?'

Truffler Mason was alerted by the mention of the name. 'Haydon Brighouse? What's he got to do with anything?'

'He is "Snowy",' said Mrs Pargeter.

'Blimey. Yes, that would figure, though, when you think about it. But what's this about him publishing lies?'

'He's got to be stopped from doing it.' Mrs Pargeter turned the full beam of her eyes on to Truffler. 'Actually, you've probably got more experience of stopping people from doing things than I have.' She said into the phone, 'Erin, I'm going to pass you over to Truffler. All well with you?'

'Fine, thanks,' said the girl.

'Good. Lots of love – and thanks for your detective work on identifying "Snowy". Here's Truffler.'

She passed the phone across, and felt a glow from the warmth with which the private investigator greeted his surrogate daughter. Erin quickly brought him up to speed with what she had told Mrs Pargeter.

Truffler Mason rubbed his chin ruefully. 'I've always been afraid something like this would happen.'

'Something like what?' asked Erin.

'Someone getting too nosey about the late Mr Pargeter's business affairs.' He caught a look from Mrs Pargeter and hastily continued, 'Not of course that there was ever anything wrong with the late Mr Pargeter's business affairs, but it's so easy in this life for people to get hold of the wrong end of the stick. And, as Mrs P says, it would be disastrous if any lies about the boss ever got published.'

'Aren't there libel laws,' suggested Erin, 'to stop that kind of thing happening? Injunctions or something? Superinjunctions?'

'Trouble with libel,' said Truffler dolefully, 'is that you can't libel people who're dead.'

'Oh, I didn't know that. Well, couldn't Mrs Pargeter take out an injunction to stop publication?'

'That would depend rather on what was actually written in the book. And finding that out could be rather costly – and public. Kind of thing that might have to go to court, and then there'd be beans spilt all over the place. No, Mr Pargeter always said – and he had the services of some of the best lawyers in the country – "Keep the lawyers out of things unless it's absolutely necessary to get them involved."'

Mrs Pargeter nodded respectfully on hearing her late husband's sage advice repeated.

'OK,' said Erin. 'So what other ways do we have of stopping Haydon Brighouse from publishing?'

'I can think of a few,' replied Truffler. But he didn't mention that one of them was by stopping Haydon Brighouse from doing anything. Ever again. Such thoughts were not to be voiced within the hearing of Mrs Pargeter.

'We'll have to think about it,' he pronounced in a terminal manner. 'Incidentally, Erin . . .'

'Yes?'

'There was something I wanted to ask you about, something to do with computers?'

'Ask away.'

'Well, look, I was just in someone's house where they'd got a laptop—' no need to spell out the details of whose house – 'and on the screen they had a copy of today's *Times* crossword.'

'Nothing strange about that. You can get almost all daily papers online these days.'

'So I gather, but the thing was, when I touched something on the laptop, another screen came up.'

'What did it look like?'

Truffler started out on the minimal description he'd treated Mrs Pargeter to, but before he'd got a sentence into it, Erin said, 'That sounds like Skype.'

'Skype?'

'Really, Truffler, it's about time you came into the twenty-first century. Skype is a means of having conversations with people when you can actually see them.'

'Like a sort of video-phone?'

'Exactly.'

'So you can see the person you're talking to on your laptop?'

'Laptop, tablet, mobile phone, all those devices.'

'Oh,' said Truffler Mason. And only people who knew him very well would have recognized how excited he was as, lugubriously, he continued, 'So someone could be seen by someone else a long way away while they gave them instructions about how to do a complicated job . . .?'

'Certainly.'

'. . . a complicated job like breaking into a safe?'

'Shouldn't be a problem,' said Erin.

Mrs Pargeter was getting a little frustrated by only hearing one end of the ongoing conversation. 'Might I have another quick word?' she asked.

Truffler said his goodbyes to Erin and passed the mobile across. As he did so, he said with satisfaction, 'Skype. Skype's how Tumblers done it.'

'Skype,' Mrs Pargeter echoed, once again talking to Erin. 'That's that thing where you can see people when you're talking to them on the phone?'

'Yes. It'd be very useful for you to use it while you're out there, actually.'

'Is it easy to arrange?' asked Mrs Pargeter cautiously. Though not quite such a technophobe as Truffler, she hadn't made many excursions into the digital world.

Erin Jarvis very quickly and simply told her how to download Skype on to her phone.

'Right. I'll try that the minute we finish this call. I was just thinking, though, Erin . . .'

'Yes?'

'If Haydon Brighouse was the one who laid that "Snowy" clue on ClinkedIn because he wanted to do some research into my husband's business affairs . . .'

'Mm?'

'. . . then there's a very good chance that it was Haydon Brighouse who stole the little black book from my safe in Chigwell . . . for the very same reason.'

'I think you're right, Mrs Pargeter,' said Erin.

TWENTY

The day's synchronicities continued. Hardly had the call ended – and before Mrs Pargeter could download Skype – the mobile rang again. It was Gary. 'How are you, Mrs P?' he asked solicitously.

'I'm fine,' she replied. 'Enjoying the Greek sun. But why're you calling? Any problems?'

'Just something I thought you ought to know about. Truffler, and all.'

'What is it?'

'I've been approached by somebody called Haydon Brighouse . . .'

'Oh yes?' There seemed to be an inevitability in what she was about to hear. 'What did he want?'

'He's been asking me questions about your husband.'

'Oh dear.'

'Says he's researching a book about him and his rivalry with the Lambeth Walkers.'

'I'm afraid I don't know what you're talking about, Gary.'

The chauffeur quickly covered his lapse. 'The detail's not important, Mrs P. What matters is how this bloke got on to me; how he knew I had anything to do with your husband. I thought those tracks had been well covered, but if he's talking about the Lambeth Walkers, then that must mean he knows—'

Again Mrs Pargeter claimed ignorance of what he was talking about. 'Maybe I should pass you over to Truffler . . .?' she suggested. 'He knows more about my husband's business affairs than I do.'

'Yeah, right. Good idea,' said Gary.

And Truffler Mason was quickly involved in a conversation, whose details Mrs Pargeter consciously tuned out.

But a grim conclusion was forming in her mind. If Haydon Brighouse had got on to Gary, he could get on to a lot more of her late husband's associates. He had contacts for all of them.

In other words, Gary's call had confirmed that Haydon Brighouse was almost definitely in possession of the little black book.

The next few hours confirmed Mrs Pargeter's worst fears. The mobile rang time after time.

Parvez the Peterman had been approached by Haydon Brighouse. So had another expert lock man, 'Keyhole Crabbe'. 'Hedgeclipper' Clinton had had a call at Greene's Hotel. 'Ankle-deep' Arkwright, also in the hospitality business, had been questioned too. 'Concrete' Jacket, texted on the site of a house he was building, had been left a message.

The list went on.

Mrs Pargeter was no longer in any doubt about it. Haydon Brighouse had got the little black book.

TWENTY-ONE

Truffler Mason looked on ruefully as Mrs Pargeter downloaded Skype on to her phone. Erin's instructions had been simple to follow. Truffler almost found himself thinking that perhaps he should get more up to date with modern technology. But that wasn't the main cause of his ruefulness. He felt he had let Mrs Pargeter down. He should have kept a closer watch on her; he should never have allowed the Chigwell house and its safe to be broken into. And, by letting down Mrs Pargeter, he was also letting down the memory of her husband.

'There – that's all loaded successfully,' she said. Though undoubtedly cast down by the course events were taking, it took more than that to dilute her cheery outlook on the world. 'Well, Truffler, it looks to me as if there's little more we can do here on Atmos. We must get back to England as soon as possible. That's where it's all going on.'

'You're right. I'll get on to HRH and make the arrangements.'

'Yes. One thing . . .'

'What?'

'The first bit, from here to Skiathos; you'd better ask him to organize some other form of transport.'

Truffler nodded, taking her point immediately. 'Of course. We want to avoid the attentions of Apostolos Philippoussis.'

'Of all the Philippoussis cousins. I get the feeling they are not on our side.' For a moment Mrs Pargeter did look downcast. 'You know what worries me?'

'What?'

'All those phone calls we've just had, from people Haydon Brighouse tried to contact, they were all loyal to my late husband's memory?'

'Of course. We all are.'

'And none of them would ever give away any information about him that . . . that might be misinterpreted?'

'No way.'

'But, on the other hand, we know there are names in that little black book of people who have turned out to be less than loyal to my husband.'

'Yes. Julian Embridge?' Truffler suggested. '"Wirecutters" Wilson?'

'And maybe others,' said Mrs Pargeter gloomily.

'Possible,' Truffler agreed. 'There isn't the loyalty around now that there was when I was growing up. So few people have any moral standards these days.' He shook his head at the wickedness of the world.

'But, Truffler, if Haydon Brighouse gets on to some of those disloyal people . . . well, they're going to feed him all kinds of shameless lies about my husband's business activities.'

'Too true.' Truffler Mason's voice plumbed new depths of lugubriousness.

'So he's got to be stopped,' said Mrs Pargeter, regaining her customary firmness and optimism. 'And he will be stopped.'

'Yes, of course he will,' said Truffler in funereal tones. 'I'll get on to HRH straight away to sort out the transport back.'

Taking out his own mobile phone, he walked out of the hotel gates and a little way down the stony road to make his call. He didn't want to announce their change of plans to the entire Philippoussis family.

Meanwhile Mrs Pargeter racked her brains for something useful she could do while she was still on Atmos. It was evening now, the sinking sun purpling the blue of the Mediterranean to a new darkness. A waiter, almost definitely another Philippoussis cousin, wearing the family moustache, came to take their drinks order. White wine for her, and Mrs Pargeter knew that Truffler would want a large Mythos beer. The waiter also asked if they would be dining in the hotel.

Mrs Pargeter looked questioningly across at Truffler, who had finished his call and was returning to the table. 'Six in the morning,' he said shortly. 'We'll be picked up by the harbour.'

So the answer to the waiter's enquiry was 'Yes'. There was a taverna down by the sea, but when they'd walked past it, they'd seen that the owner was yet another Philippoussis cousin. Wherever they went on Atmos, they'd be under surveillance. So dining in the Hotel Thalassa was no more of a security risk than anywhere else.

'Would you like to eat out here?' the waiter asked. They were sitting at one of the terrace tables nearest to the harbour.

'Yes, it's very pleasant,' said Mrs Pargeter. 'We can watch the sunset.' The evening light-show would be spectacular, particularly when the last curve of the purple sun was seen through the frame of the Widowmaker rock.

'Very good,' said the waiter. 'I will bring menus when I bring your drinks.'

After the waiter had left, Mrs Pargeter suddenly had an idea. 'Ellie Fenchurch!' she announced.

Truffler Mason knew who she meant. 'What about her?'

Ellie had been a teenager with aspirations to becoming a journalist when the late Mr Pargeter had taken her under his wing. He had encouraged her career ambitions and fixed work for her as a cub reporter on local newspapers. He had also taught her a lot about the dark arts of Public Relations, and in fact Ellie had acted for him in that capacity. There are far too many people out in the world far too ready to blacken the reputation of a major player in Mr Pargeter's areas of enterprise. It was frequently necessary for someone to get into newspapers stories of his philanthropy and charitable works. And Ellie Fenchurch had proved to be very adept at such tasks.

'She's a journalist. She might know about Haydon Brighouse. She might have some dirt on him.'

With the synchronicity to which Mrs Pargeter was becoming accustomed, at that moment her mobile phone rang. And of course at the other end was Ellie Fenchurch.

'Do you know a little toerag called Haydon Brighouse?' the husky Cockney voice demanded.

'Funny, Ellie, I was about to ask you exactly the same question. It's strange how important that name has suddenly become to us out here.'

'Who's "us" and where's "out here"?'

'I am currently on the Greek island of Atmos in the company of one Truffler Mason.'

'Blimey, what're you doing out there?'

Mrs Pargeter started to explain, but was interrupted by Ellie saying, 'It'd be easier to do this if I could see you. Do you by any chance Skype?'

'Oh yes,' Mrs Pargeter replied airily, as if she'd had the app on her phone for years rather than minutes.

Ellie said she'd call back. Mrs Pargeter followed the instructions Erin had given her and within minutes she could see the journalist's face, long like the rest of her angular body. The hair was currently cut very short and the purple of a Stanley plum.

'Nice to see you, Mrs P,' said Ellie. 'Move the phone back a bit so's I can see where you are.' Mrs Pargeter obeyed the instruction. 'Ooh, lovely sunset you've got there. And Truffler's looking very relaxed.'

'Actually, Ellie, we're neither of us at all relaxed. Things are getting rather uncomfortable out here.'

'And is that in any way due to the aforementioned Haydon Brighouse?'

'It certainly is.'

'I'm not surprised. He was sniffing round me, asking about the old days when I worked with Mr Pargeter.'

'Yes, he's been doing that with a lot of my husband's former business associates.'

'How's he got our contacts?'

'I'm afraid he's got hold of the little black book.' And Mrs Pargeter proceeded to bring Ellie Fenchurch up to speed with everything that had been happening in the last few weeks. She concluded, 'And I was wondering if you knew anything about him, you know, as a fellow journalist?'

'Only things I have found out about him suggest that to call him a journalist is overstating the case. He's nothing more than a muck-raker, devoted to besmirching the names of celebrities.'

Some people might have thought this criticism a bit rich, coming from the mouth of someone whose claim to fame was her national Sunday newspaper interview in which every week another eminent reputation was ritually shredded. But Mrs Pargeter didn't think that, and if she had she certainly wouldn't have said anything.

'Well, look, Ellie, I want you to find out everything you can about Haydon Brighouse.'

'Don't worry, I was about to do that, anyway.'

'Obviously if you can get any dirt on him, that's good. But also try to find out if he's got a publisher lined up for this book he's currently researching.'

'I'm sure he has. He's done exposés on the Krays and the Richardsons, which have sold quite well among the kind of pond life who enjoy reading True Crime, so if he's planning to do something about the rivalry between your husband's gang and the Lambeth Walkers, then I'm sure he'll—'

'Sorry,' said Mrs Pargeter, 'but I don't know what you're talking about.'

Something in her tone made Ellie change tack. 'No, well, of course you wouldn't, Mrs P. Don't worry, I'll get the full

SP on Haydon Brighouse – you just leave it with me. And enjoy the rest of your holiday.'

'Truffler and I aren't on holiday. I'll be back in Chigwell some time tomorrow.'

'Right,' said Ellie. 'Very soon I will bombard you with information about Haydon Brighouse.'

'Great.'

Shortly after the end of the Skype call, the Philippoussis cousin who was acting as waiter came out to lay a paper cloth on their table, tucking the ends under elastic to keep it in place should the wind get up. He proffered menus to the pair of them.

The range of dishes was surprisingly varied. There is a general rule that the further a Greek island is from the main-land and the smaller it is, the less inventive are its menus. But on Atmos the choice was considerable. The prices were consid-erable too. Mrs Pargeter deduced that Mendy Farstairs was not the only well-heeled foreign villa-owner on the island.

She ordered mixed mezes and moussaka. Truffler, who had a proper Englishman's distrust of foreign food, said he would forgo a starter, and homed in on a pork chop with chips. 'And no sauces,' he told the waiter suspiciously, 'unless you've got some ketchup.'

'Yes, of course, sir, we have ketchup. A lot of English and American guests come to the Hotel Thalassa.'

When the food arrived it was remarkably good. But though Mrs Pargeter put away the best part of a bottle of white wine and Truffler dealt with a couple more large Mythos beers, they didn't talk much over the meal. Partly that was for security reasons. They didn't want to talk about anything important in the middle of the Philippoussis surveillance network, and the only things they did want to talk about were important. It was no time for small talk. So neither of them said much.

The minds of both were full of their own thoughts. Mrs Pargeter was slightly anxious about how they would make their getaway the following morning. Packing their bags and refusing to travel in one of Apostolos Philippoussis's speedboats would surely set alarm bells ringing right through Atmos. Still, she hadn't had any opportunity to ask Truffler about the phone call in which he'd made the arrangements. No doubt HRH had worked out an exit strategy for them. He was good at that kind of thing. In fact, getting people out of threatening circumstances was one of his greatest areas of expertise. As both Lord Lucan and Shergar could attest.

But Mrs Pargeter's other cause for anxiety was the fact that their trip to Atmos had yielded so little in the way of information. True, they had deduced that Tumblers Tate had instructed someone – probably on Skype – how to get into her safe. And it also seemed a likely deduction that the perpetrator was Haydon Brighouse.

Now she came to think of it, where was Haydon's mother? According to her personal assistant, Rochelle Brighouse was also supposed to be on Atmos. Where, wondered Mrs Pargeter.

She had a nagging, guilty sensation of unfinished business.

And she got the impression that Truffler was feeling the same. Though she refused coffee because she didn't want it to keep her awake, he downed two large espressos. When he had finished the second he rose from the table. Picking up his raincoat, he said ponderously, 'I think I'll go and have a stroll on the beach before I turn in.'

TWENTY-TWO

She couldn't sleep. It wasn't the heat. Amongst Hotel Thalassa's modern amenities there was, of course, state-of-the-art air conditioning. And her bed couldn't have been more comfortable. Her nightdress was just the right weight as well. But Mrs Pargeter felt restless, deprived of the soothing unconsciousness into which she normally slipped so easily. For a woman like her, who had never done anything in her life that might have caused the smallest twinge of guilt, deep sleep was something that she had always taken for granted.

But that night it wouldn't come. Partly it was anxiety about Truffler. Though he hadn't spelt out his intentions, she was in no doubt that his 'stroll on the beach' was going to take him back to Tumblers Tate's cottage. And after the private investigator's first visit, she felt pretty sure that the Philippoussis family would be watching out for him. He was definitely tempting providence.

And while she had infinite faith in Truffler Mason's sleuthing skills, she didn't feel so confident of his abilities if the situation became violent. He was strong but no longer a young man and was likely to find himself outnumbered.

So she found herself waiting for the sound of Truffler letting himself into his room like an anxious mother whose son, having just passed his driving test, was out for his first evening alone in the car.

But she knew it wasn't just anxiety about Truffler that was disturbing her. The feeling that she'd had earlier on the hotel terrace, that her investigations on Atmos were somehow incomplete, had returned to her with redoubled force. It was mad to have come so far and to return to England with such meagre pickings. She felt certain that the PhiliPussies cat sanctuary had more secrets to divulge.

The unaccustomed mental distress was actually making her head ache, and Mrs Pargeter, who normally eschewed all medication, found herself rooting in her handbag for some paracetamol. As she did so, her hand closed round an unfamiliar small plastic object.

She had forgotten all about it, but as she brought the device out into the light, she remembered what Parvez the Peterman had said when he gave it to her. 'All you need to know, Mrs P, is that if you direct this towards any padlock in the world – even electronic ones or ones with a numerical code – the padlock will instantly open.'

She started to get dressed again.

The Padlock Pass did everything Parvez the Peterman had promised it would. From the balcony of her bedroom, a convenient wrought-iron spiral staircase led down to the Hotel Thalassa's pool area, and Mrs Pargeter had negotiated that with commendable silence. There were no lights on in the main building – or indeed anywhere else that she could see. Villa Rufus too was closed down for the night. It took a few moments for her eyes to accommodate, but soon she could see quite clearly in the minimal moonlight. For the first time since she had arrived on Atmos, she felt pretty sure that her movements were unobserved.

The night air was heavy, still warm on her skin, and redolent of pine resin and thyme. There were few sounds, just the recalcitrant creak of boats at anchor and the rattle of metal rigging against masts down at the harbour. From far away the occasional dog barked and, more pertinently, there was some distant feline yowling from her destination.

Mrs Pargeter stepped over the low stone wall which marked the boundaries of Villa Rufus, and advanced past the pool, through the ancient colonnades towards the enclosure at the back.

Her memory had not failed her. The wrought-iron gates at the front were secured by a chain through whose links a large and efficient-looking padlock was fixed. She raised Parvez the Peterman's device, pointed it in the right direction and pressed the green button. With a loud metallic click the padlock immediately sprang open.

Having used the Padlock Pass's red button to reclose the gate and hide the fact of her entrance, Mrs Pargeter advanced into the compound.

The yowling of the cats did not increase significantly with the presence of an intruder in their midst. Their level of complaint continued pretty much the same day and night. They regarded all human beings as their enemies, people who had taken them away from the delightful filth and smells of the harbourside and locked them up. It would take a lot of argument (assuming cats could understand argument) to persuade them that PhiliPussies was a charity whose aim was actually to make their lives better.

As she moved further into the sanctuary, Mrs Pargeter noticed that there were a lot of security cameras around. But the thought that her every move might be being recorded did not worry her. She doubted whether there was anyone actually monitoring the live footage of her actions. Somebody might well check through the tape the following morning, but at six o'clock she and Truffler would be heading away from Atmos in the alternative transport HRH had arranged for them. She felt safe.

She also knew exactly where she wanted to go in the PhiliPussies compound. She had no interest in the cats in their cages. They could continue their disgruntled wailing; she wouldn't pay them any attention.

What did interest her was the spotless, state-of-the-art surgery that Costas Philippoussis had showed her with such pride. There was something she had seen there – or perhaps something that she hadn't seen during her tour – that intrigued her. She found the right building with no problem. The metal door was locked with a hefty padlock. Mrs Pargeter pointed Parvez the Peterman's invention straight at it and pressed the button.

Instantly the padlock clicked open, and hung, swaying slightly, from its ring. She disengaged it from the hasp and went inside.

Though unconcerned by the security cameras, she still thought switching the lights on would be a risk too far, so she extracted the LED torch from her handbag and, pointing it downwards, let the thin, strong beam illuminate her way ahead.

Her destination was the stainless steel table in the centre of the room. She remembered Costas Philippoussis's slight change of manner when she'd asked him about microchipping the cats. He had become defensive when the subject was mentioned.

She ran the beam of her torch over the surface of the table. It was spotlessly clean. Whatever surgery might have taken place there during the day, all traces of it had been hygienically removed.

Inspecting the table more closely, Mrs Pargeter saw that along each side were rows of drawers, also made of stainless steel. She opened one at random. It was full of bandages and dressings. Another revealed a variety of gags and tubing, presumably to enable cats to breathe normally while under anaesthetic.

But the contents of the third drawer Mrs Pargeter slid open were rather different. They were two rectangular boxes made of dull grey metal. As she tried to lift one, its weight suggested that it was made of lead. Each of the boxes was closed by a small padlock.

Once again, out of the handbag came Parvez the Peterman's little gizmo. It was directed at one of the boxes, a quick zap and the padlock sprang open. Mrs Pargeter lifted the lid.

What she saw inside the box was a collection of small pellets, each one maybe half an inch long. They were made of some dark substance that looked and felt like metal or possibly ceramic. Mrs Pargeter tried to imagine what possible medical function the pellets might serve for feline ailments, but she couldn't think of anything. They were much too big to be microchips.

She picked up two or three of the pellets and put them in her handbag. Then her attention was drawn through the window by the sight of torch beams approaching the surgery block.

Thank God, she thought, for the Padlock Pass's second function, its ability to relock the padlocks it had just opened. No delay fumbling with closing the surgery door. A quick press on the red button the moment she was outside and all signs of her entering the block had been covered up. By the time the torch beams reached the surgery she was safely hidden round the corner of an adjacent building.

There were two torches, held by two people. Before she could actually see them in the gloom, Mrs Pargeter identified them by their voices.

'I just thought it would interest you . . .' It was a woman talking, a woman she immediately recognized as Rochelle Brighouse. 'I know it's nothing to do with the case you're working on, but any evidence of criminal activity is always interesting.'

'Couldn't agree more, Mum.' Even without his use of the final word, Mrs Pargeter would have known it was Haydon. 'Possibilities of blackmail . . .?'

'You never know your luck, Haydon. Besides, you know

that when you're investigating a crime it stops you from indulging in your other little habit that—'

'Let's get this place open,' said the young man brusquely, unwilling for his mother to pursue her current topic. 'Have you got the key to the padlock?'

'Of course I have, Haydon.' There was a scrape of metal against metal and a certain amount of jiggling. The use of a key was much less efficient than Parvez the Peterman's device.

But eventually the metal door swung open.

'Right. You show me,' said Haydon Brighouse. 'But I should warn you, Mum, I can only really concentrate on one story at a time.'

'I know that, love.'

'And the story I'm concentrating on at the moment is getting all the dirt I can on the late Mr Pargeter.'

In spite of the balmy Grecian night, Mrs Pargeter found herself shivering.

TWENTY-THREE

As Mrs Pargeter had anticipated, Truffler Mason's 'stroll on the beach' took him straight to Tumblers Tate's cottage. The moon was slightly fuller than it had been on his previous visit and he could see everything very clearly, though moonlight had drained the blue colour out of the door.

Truffler raised a hand to knock, but then decided to try the latch. The door was unlocked. He pushed his way in.

The front room and the kitchen were in darkness, but soft light glowed from the terrace at the end. Truffler Mason advanced until he was standing in the doorway, looking out at the lounger on which Tumblers Tate lay in exactly the same pose as he had on their last encounter. Of Theodosia – or any of her Philippoussis cousins – there was no sign.

This time Tumblers Tate made no pretence that he was suffering from dementia. Maybe he only did that when there were witnesses. He didn't attempt to shift from his recumbent position, but he waved a thin hand towards his visitor and said, 'I thought I might see you again. Our last conversation was somewhat interrupted.'

'You could say that,' Truffler agreed.

'In fact I was so sure you'd be coming back . . .' The old man gestured to the table at his side, '. . . that I put out another brandy balloon for you. Take a seat.'

Truffler did as instructed, hanging his raincoat over the back of the chair, and watched while Tumblers poured a drink for him. Though the old man's movements were slow, his clawlike hands showed not the slightest tremor.

The source of illumination was a single bulkhead light whose metal cage had yielded its original blackness to rust. It was fixed to the sheer rock which backed the terrace. Around it buzzed the usual line-up of houseflies, mosquitos and kamikaze moths.

Tumblers gestured towards the insect throng as he passed the brandy across. 'I'm afraid you're likely to get bitten to death out here.'

'I'll survive,' said Truffler.

The old man let out a dry cackle. 'Me they don't bother about. Can't find enough skin on me to get a decent bite.' He took a generous slurp of brandy before continuing. And when he did speak, his words had the quality of a prepared speech. 'Listen, I've been thinking quite a lot since I last saw you . . .'

Truffler didn't interrupt, allowing Tumblers to pace his own narrative. 'Thing is, it may sound like stating the obvious, but I am now very old. Not going to be long before I snuff it.'

Truffler didn't offer any words of denial or condolence. Tumblers Tate was speaking no less than the truth.

'And I've been thinking . . . I'm quite proud of what I've achieved . . . you know, professionally.'

'So you should be. No one's going to argue with the fact that you're the best living cracksman . . . even if you did always work for the wrong side.'

'Yeah, I been thinking about that too, the time I spent with the Lambeth Walkers . . . and some of the things that happened there . . . well, I'm not so proud of them.'

'Like what?'

'There was always a lot of violence around when the Lambeth Walkers done a job.'

'Certainly was. They was famous for it.'

'And at the time I kind of went along with it, because, you know, that's how they worked and at my end of the business I didn't have to be too hands-on about that stuff. But a lot of people got hurt . . . unnecessarily.'

'How'dja mean? I'm sure the Lambeth Walkers thought it was necessary at the time.'

'Oh yes, they did. No doubt about that. But a lot of it was just frightening people for the sake of frightening them.'

'Well, it worked, didn't it?' Truffler Mason found himself in the strange position of almost defending the Lambeth Walkers, Mr Pargeter's most bitter enemies.

'Anyway,' Tumblers Tate continued, 'I don't feel too good about some of what happened.'

'Water under the bridge,' Truffler suggested.

'It was the bodies under the bridge that bothered me more. Not to mention the bodies that ended up in the cement pillars of motorway bridges.'

'That was a different time,' Truffler reassured. 'And as you say, you weren't directly involved in the violence.'

'I was involved by association,' Tumblers insisted.

His visitor shrugged. 'No point in beating yourself up about it now.'

'But I do beat myself up about it. I lie awake nights – the brandy ought to knock me out, but it doesn't – and I think about the big disappointment of my life.'

'What was that then?' Truffler asked gingerly. He didn't want to invite confessions about the old man's failed relationships.

'The big disappointment of my life was that I worked for the Lambeth Walkers and not for Mr Pargeter.'

Surprise caused a moment's silence before Truffler Mason said, 'Ah, yes, well, I can see that.'

'There was almost never any violence around Mr Pargeter's operations.'

'No, there wasn't. Except when it was absolutely necessary.'

'Yes, whereas with the Lambeth Walkers, soon as they saw

an opportunity to hurt someone . . .' The old man shook his head despairingly. 'I'd have given anything to have been Mr Pargeter's cracksman.'

'Did you ever let him know that?'

'No. By the time I'd realized what I really wanted to do, I was too caught up with the Lambeth Walkers. If they'd ever found out I was thinking of defecting . . . well, I wouldn't be talking to you here now.'

'No,' agreed Truffler, remembering some of the things that had happened to Lambeth Walkers whose loyalty had become suspect.

'And now Mr Pargeter's dead,' said Tumblers Tate gloomily, 'and I'll be dead soon, and I can't show him the respect that I always felt for him.'

'No,' said Truffler. He spoke slowly, but his thoughts were making connections fast. 'Of course, Tumblers, there are still things you could do that would show your appreciation for the late Mr Pargeter.'

'Oh yes?'

'You could help out his widow.'

A smile wreathed the old man's face. 'Yes, that'd be good. I'd never thought about his widow. I guess I'd heard that he was married, but I didn't know his missus was still alive.'

'She's very much alive,'

'Yes, if I could help her . . .'

Truffler couldn't stop himself from saying, 'Well, what you've done so far has been rather the reverse of helping her.'

Tumblers Tate looked puzzled. 'I'm sorry. I don't know what you're talking about. I've never had anything to do with Mr Pargeter's widow.'

'No? You've only broken into her safe.'

'What?'

'Do you deny that, within the last week, you have used Skype to instruct someone how to break into a safe in a house in Chigwell?'

'No, I don't deny that. Lovely bit of work, that was. Parvez the Peterman must've designed that. There's no one else out there with that level of sophistication.'

'It was Parvez who done it.'

'Course it was. I knew I was right.'

'And are you telling me that you didn't know the house with the safe belonged to Mr Pargeter's widow?'

'I hadn't got a clue about that. I'd never have done it if I'd known. No, I was only called on the Skype once the perpetrator was right up close to the house. So I didn't see much of it.'

'And you instructed the perpetrator on Skype about how to break in without leaving any signs of forcible entry?'

'I certainly did.'

'And you told him how to get into the safe?'

'Yes.'

'What I can't understand is how you broke through the final security barrier. Surely that required Mrs Pargeter's thumbprint to open it?'

The old man chuckled. 'I have ways of cloning prints.'

'How?'

Tumblers Tate looked beadily at Truffler. 'You hoping I'm going to tell you all my trade secrets?'

'No. No, of course not.'

'Good. That safe, you know, it was a work of art. As I say, Parvez the Peterman didn't make my job easy. Respect where it's due, he's a bright boy, that one. When I kick the bucket, he'll be top of the league, no question.'

'So,' asked Truffler, 'who was it you gave the instructions to, you know, about opening the safe?'

'Ah, well, it was—'

'No, let me guess.' Truffler played the pause for all it was worth. 'Haydon Brighouse?'

'Got it in one.'

'I thought so. So it was Haydon who contacted you and set the whole thing up?'

'No, he only broke into the house and opened the safe. It was all set up by—'

Once again he was stopped by a raised hand from Truffler. 'No, let me guess this one too. The whole thing was set up by Haydon's mother, Rochelle Brighouse!'

'You're on a roll, Truffler. Dead right.'

An almost imperceptible twitch of a smile showed the private investigator's wild elation. 'And did you know, Tumblers, what Haydon Brighouse wanted out of the safe?'

'No. Money, jewellery, the usual stuff, I imagine.'

Truffler couldn't see any point in telling the old cracksman about the little black book. Instead, he asked, 'So, is Rochelle Brighouse a crook then?'

'And how! Apparently now she has this Public Relations agency as a front, but she's still up to her neck in crime. Her husband died and all, like Mr Pargeter, but that didn't stop Rochelle. She carried on the business from where he left off.'

'So what was her husband's name?'

'Well, she was married twice. First one was called Bernie Brighouse.'

'Haydon's dad?'

'That's right. And a total waste of space he was. Rochelle divorced him when Haydon was just a nipper, but she kept the surname 'cause she'd already set up her Public Relations company under that name. Then she married Gordon Edwards.'

'Never heard of him,' said Truffler, puzzled. His knowledge of the criminal underworld was usually comprehensive.

'Ah, no. Well, he didn't use that name, Gordon Edwards, professionally.'

'So what was his work monicker?'

'Knuckles Norton.'

Truffler Mason's shock was so great that almost a full minute went past before he could speak. When they finally came out, his words were, 'So Rochelle Brighouse was married to the boss of the Lambeth Walkers?'

Tumblers Tate confirmed that this was the case. Truffler was again silent as he worked out the ramifications of the revelation. No wonder the late Mr Pargeter and his sister hadn't seen a lot of each other. They were deadly rivals, and now that rivalry was being continued in a different way between their widows. Truffler couldn't wait to hear Mrs Pargeter's reaction when she heard the news.

'So,' he finally managed to ask, 'what kind of crime is Rochelle Brighouse involved in now?'

The old man's mouth twisted in a grimace of distaste. 'Things I don't approve of. When I was working with the

Lambeth Walkers, yes, there was too much violence, but the crimes we were committing were good, honest, old-fashioned stuff . . . basically stealing money and jewels and that. We never got involved in gun-running or arming terrorists.'

'And is that what Rochelle and Haydon Brighouse are doing?'

'Haydon doesn't do anything more than what his mum tells him. He's a very weak personality. But Rochelle's got herself into some pretty dark stuff.'

'Haydon's some kind of journalist, isn't he?'

'Yes. He's trying to write something about the turf wars between the Lambeth Walkers and your lot.'

'I heard that. Has he been on to you for information?'

'Oh yes.'

'And did you give him any?'

'Oh no. Truffler, whatever else I may be, I am at heart an old-fashioned criminal. And one thing an old-fashioned criminal never does is grass up his mates.'

'Couldn't agree more. So Haydon's not a major player in his mum's current activities?'

'No. She likes to keep a close eye on him, though, because of certain behavioural problems he has.'

'What kind of—?'

But Tumblers Tate wasn't listening. 'I've been thinking . . . what you said about me maybe doing a good turn for Mr Pargeter's widow . . .'

'Yes?'

'I've thought of something I could do to help her.'

'What?'

'Look, like I said, as an old-fashioned criminal, I'd never grass anyone up, but that doesn't mean I wouldn't shop someone who was perpetrating the kind of crime I disapprove of.'

Truffler caught on immediately. 'Like, let us say . . . Rochelle Brighouse?'

The old man grinned. 'Exactly. I've got a whole dossier of evidence against her.'

'Where?'

'I'll show you. This, Truffler, is my *pièce de résistance*, the greatest creation of my career as a cracksman and safe designer. You think you encountered state-of-the-art . . . You wait till you've seen this.'

He pressed something on the underside of his lounger and suddenly in the rock wall that backed the terrace two parallel cracks appeared where the surface had shown no cracks before. A large rectangular chunk of stone projected forwards and slid away like the side door of a van, revealing a subtly lit cell rather bigger than the cottage's kitchen.

'Blimey!' said Truffler. 'How does that work?'

'That's my secret,' said Tumblers Tate with a sly grin. 'There's more than eighty years' experience of being a cracksman gone into that design. Tell you, it's more secure than Fort Knox, that little baby is.' He pointed to the cell's walls, all of which were lined with shiny metal shelves on which stood ranks of shiny metal files. 'Entire history of my life in there, Truffler. Evidence that could bring down some of the biggest villains in the world.' He pressed some other remote and a spotlight picked out one vertical column of files. 'And that lot is all evidence of the crimes of Knuckles Norton.' The light narrowed its focus to one particular shelf. 'While that is the information which could ensure that his widow Rochelle Brighouse spent the rest of her days at Her Majesty's pleasure.'

'Can I have a look?' asked Truffler Mason.

'Of course.' Tumblers Tate gestured towards the cell's interior. 'Go inside, by all means.'

And the private investigator did as was suggested.

TWENTY-FOUR

Back in her bed at Hotel Thalassa, Mrs Pargeter was not relaxed. Sleep continued to evade her. Partly her mind was full of the possibilities opened up by the snatch of conversation she had heard from Rochelle Brighouse and her son.

But, more than that, as the hours dragged past, she worried increasingly about Truffler.

Truffler raised his head from the open file he was reading. 'Pretty inflammatory stuff here, Tumblers.'

'You can say that again.'

'And you don't mind my using it, getting the information into the ears of the right people?'

'Can't think of anything I'd like better, Truffler. Like I say, I'm disappointed in myself about some of the things I got up to when I was working with the Lambeth Walkers. Stitching up Rochelle Brighouse would be a kind of payback for me, make me think I've done some good with my life before I snuff it.'

'Good for you, Tumblers.' Truffler looked admiringly round the cell in which he was standing. 'This place is absolutely brilliant.'

'Yes.' The old cracksman smiled complacently. 'Though I say it myself, I reckon I done a good job there.'

'You certainly did. When it's closed, nobody'd ever find it, would they?'

'No. There's some pretty crafty electronics in there. Though I was very impressed with what Parvez the Peterman had done with that safe in Chigwell, that's still a few steps behind what I've done with this little baby here.'

'And presumably it's personalized, not just electronic codes and stuff . . .?'

'You're right. The final key to opening it is my own thumbprint.'

'Same method Parvez used in Chigwell. So you just press your thumb on that pad on the lounger?'

'That's it. A half-competent cracksman might be able to get through the electronic numbers stuff, but only my thumbprint can actually open the place.'

'And presumably nobody on the island knows that this secret cell exists?'

'Of course not,' Tumblers Tate replied contemptuously. 'You think I'm going to tell all the Philippoussises about something like that?'

'Of course you aren't.' Truffler let out a lugubrious chuckle. 'So if you snuff it, nobody will ever be able to get in?'

'Exactly.'

'Nice work, Tumblers.'

'Yes, bloody nice work.' He sloshed brandy into his glass. 'In fact, I done such a good job, I'm going to do a toast to myself.' He raised the balloon and made as if to sit up. 'Here's to Tumblers Tate, the best cracksman in the world!'

But before the old man could raise the glass to his lips, it dropped from his unfeeling hand to shatter on the stone floor of the terrace. The other ancient hand clutched at his chest.

And as, from inside the secret cell, Truffler Mason watched the heavy rock door slide back into place, he realized that Tumblers Tate had indeed snuffed it.

TWENTY-FIVE

Mrs Pargeter was suffering severe misgivings as she quietly packed her bag at the end of her sleepless vigil. She had seen no sign of Truffler, but his last instructions to her had been to be down at the harbour at 'six in the morning' to meet the transport that HRH had arranged. So, unable to think of any other viable course of action, she set off down to the harbour in time for a six o'clock pick-up.

As the final act of her packing, Mrs Pargeter had transferred a couple of items from her handbag into the capacious security of her bra.

The Hotel Thalassa was eerily silent. Nor did she meet anyone on her way down to the harbour. With her suitcase in one hand and her handbag in the other, she stood on the stone harbour wall waiting. The sun was beginning to rise behind her and flashed tentative light on to the archway of the Widowmaker rock opposite.

The first sign that something had gone wrong was the sight of Apostolos Philippoussis's speedboat entering the harbour, towing another speedboat whose front windows had been pierced by what looked like bullet holes.

Mrs Pargeter turned and saw – advancing from the village towards her – Costa, Vasilis, Yannis and other moustached waiters and boatmen. Even Theodosia had joined them.

To Mrs Pargeter, it seemed as though there were Philippoussis cousins as far as the eye could see.

TWENTY-SIX

Truffler Mason was profoundly frustrated. Though the door of the secret cell had closed, locking him in, the interior light had stayed on. Gloomily he checked his mobile phone and was unsurprised to see that there was no signal from his location in the middle of the living rock.

Without hope he looked around his prison. Someone with Tumblers Tate's level of skill was not likely to have left another exit unlocked. In fact, someone with Tumblers Tate's skills would have ensured that there wasn't another exit. And there wasn't.

The only surprise yielded by his survey of the scene was an envelope lying on a table. It was addressed to Parvez the Peterman. Maybe inside was some important information that Tumblers Tate had intended to post to his rival. Truffler didn't open the envelope to find out. It wasn't addressed to him, and he had high old-fashioned standards about reading other people's mail.

The light in the cell enabled him to see on its shelves the vast store of data that the late Tumblers Tate had accumulated during his long working life. Truffler knew how valuable all that evidence would be in solving a multitude of crimes and bringing a multitude of villains to justice.

He also knew that he would never be able to pass over the data to the proper authorities. No one knew of the existence of the vault in which he was incarcerated. And even if anyone did know, the place could not be opened except by its recognizing the unique thumbprint of the late Tumblers Tate. And the chances of Tumblers Tate's corpse being left *in situ* for long after Theodosia arrived at the cottage in the morning were rather smaller than the chances of a Premier League footballer being able to speak English.

Truffler Mason was not given to sentimentality, least of all where his own life expectancy was concerned. A man in his line of businesses, both the one before and the one after the death of Mr Pargeter, must frequently have been in situations where he might be killed, so the risk was one that he had come to terms with.

As a result, he settled down philosophically to read through Tumblers Tate's extensive archive until such time as either hunger or thirst would finish him off.

But even as he anticipated death, Truffler Mason did not lose his instincts as an investigator. The stuff he was reading was incendiary. It contained information about the Lambeth Walkers that could have sent many of their former members down for very long sentences.

So, though he didn't like using his mobile for anything other than making telephone calls, Truffler recognized the practicality of photographing some of the juicier documents. He might never be able to pass on the results of his researches in person, but at least the information could one day be extracted from his phone.

He became quite engrossed in the work. As he clicked away at incriminating record after incriminating record, his only real regret was the thought of never seeing Mrs Pargeter or Erin Jarvis again.

The Philippoussis cousins did not manhandle Mrs Pargeter back from the harbour wall. They just formed two silent lines through which she walked in the direction they wanted her to go. She knew there was no point in trying to escape.

As she set off to run the gauntlet of their disapproval, the Philippoussis cousins' destination was, it soon became clear, the cat sanctuary. But they knew a back way of getting there which would not alert Mendy Farstairs in Villa Rufus to their movements.

Still not a word had been spoken as Mrs Pargeter was led back to the surgery block where she had been only a few hours earlier. They had made no attempt to restrain her, confident in their numerical advantage.

Once inside, unwilling to be cowed by them, Mrs Pargeter pulled a chair away from the wall and sat down next to the metal table, waiting to see what would happen next.

The Philippoussis cousins also seemed to be waiting for something. Or someone.

Had Truffler Mason been able to pass on to her the information he'd received from Tumblers Tate, Mrs Pargeter would have been even more certain who they were waiting for. But, even without that knowledge, she was unsurprised when the door of the surgery opened to admit Rochelle Brighouse.

The Public Relations consultant (and so much more) had a smile of triumph on her thin face. Though they hadn't met till the PhiliPussies reception, Rochelle had resented the existence of her sister-in-law for many years. The rivalry between the late Mr Pargeter and Gordon Edwards (or Knuckles Norton) had been longstanding and vicious. To Rochelle's mind it continued with undiminished ferocity between their widows.

'So, rather on your own now, aren't you, Melita?' she said, somehow sensing how little Mrs Pargeter liked her first name to be used.

'I wouldn't be too sure of that,' came the defiant response. 'Truffler Mason's on the island too, you know.'

'If he's still on the island, Melita, we'll soon find him and neutralize any threat that he might pose. You might as well save yourself – and us – a lot of trouble by telling us where he's gone.'

Mrs Pargeter thought she might try responding with the truth . . . and a little bit of invention. 'Last night Truffler went to see Tumblers Tate . . . to get him to spill the beans on a variety of crimes which could see you sent down for a long time, Rochelle.'

The woman chuckled. It was not a pleasant sound. 'You'll have to do better than that, Melita.' But Rochelle had taken in the information and snapped out some instructions in Greek.

Theodosia and Yannis Philippoussis left the surgery, presumably to check out Tumblers Tate's cottage.

'You know,' Rochelle went on, 'you're going to be very useful to me, Melita.'

'I doubt it.'

'Oh yes, you are. To me and Haydon.'

'Your kleptomaniac son?' said Mrs Pargeter defiantly.

The adjective she'd used clearly annoyed Rochelle Brighouse. 'Haydon is not a kleptoma—'

'Oh yes, he is. It's engrained in his nature.' Mrs Pargeter took a punt on a new idea. 'And you've spent your life trying to cover up for him. Returning the gold cat necklace he stole at that PhiliPussies reception when we first met. That's been the story of your life, Rochelle.'

The expression on her adversary's face told Mrs Pargeter that her conjecture had been spot on. So did the speed with which Rochelle changed the subject. 'Anyway, Melita, the way you're going to be helpful to me is by giving lots of information about my late brother Lionel's criminal activities.'

'I know nothing about Lionel's criminal activities.' Her words were almost true.

But Rochelle was ready for that response. 'No, you may not know a lot, but you know a lot of people who are brimful of all kinds of dirt.'

'Oh?'

'I'm talking about the names in your little black book.'

'Ah. The little black book which your son stole, following instructions from Tumblers Tate.'

Rochelle was clearly taken aback by the extent of Mrs Pargeter's knowledge, but she still pressed on, 'And all of your contacts in that little black book are going to help Haydon to write his book by spilling lots of beans about my late brother's criminal activities.'

Mrs Pargeter let out a light laugh. 'Nice idea, Rochelle, but sadly not a goer. Haydon has already approached some of my contacts, and not one of them has given him the smallest crumb of information.'

'No, but that situation might change.'

'I don't see how.'

'Your contacts from the little black book are very loyal to you, aren't they?'

'To the death.'

'And they will do anything you instruct them to do?'

'Of course.'

'So if you were to tell them to give Haydon all the information he requires, they would do as they're told?'

'Undoubtedly. But there is one small point you seem not to have taken into consideration, Rochelle, and that is that never, under any circumstances, would I give them instructions to spill even the smallest bean.'

'You may think that at the moment, Melita, but there is one small point you seem not to have taken into consideration, and that is that I have ways of making you change your mind.' And before Mrs Pargeter could respond, Rochelle Brighouse barked out an order. 'Give her the butorphanol!'

Mrs Pargeter felt her arms pinioned to her sides. The short sleeves of her top made it easy for Costas Philippoussis to stab the syringe and empty its contents into her upper arm.

She tried to remonstrate but words failed to form on her lips.

And, as consciousness seeped away from her, the last thing she saw, hanging from the metal table in the surgery, was a tartan dog lead.

TWENTY-SEVEN

When she finally came round, Mrs Pargeter had no idea where she was. The inside of her mouth felt like coarse sandpaper. Her head ached cruelly and the jolting she was experiencing made her wonder whether she'd been put in a barrel and tipped over the edge of Niagara Falls.

She closed her eyes, hoping that when she next opened them her situation would be clearer.

It was. And part of her reorientation was achieved by noise.

She was aware of an amazing cacophony of caterwauling. How she'd managed to sleep through it so long was a tribute to the potency of the butorphanol. It sounded as though a couple of dozen angry cats had been locked in a tin box.

And, when she looked around, she discovered that the image was not so far from the truth. The tin box in which she and the cats were incarcerated was on wheels. In fact, it was a minivan driving over an extremely stony track.

Mrs Pargeter's mind made the connection. She felt pretty sure she must be in the vehicle in which the feral cats of Atmos were driven towards their finishing school at the PhiliPussies clinic in Leigh-on-Sea.

She very quickly identified the driver. Mrs Pargeter had no difficulty in recognizing the well-muscled back view of Costas Philippoussis.

She then checked her own position. The interior of the minivan was divided by stout metal grilles into two cages. In the front one the cats, which had a few old blankets on the floor to shield them from some of the vehicle's motion, yowled and complained. A couple of trays of cat litter had been laid out for their use, but the evidence on the floor – and the smell – suggested that cat litter represented a level of sophistication that they had not yet aspired to.

Some of the animals, Mrs Pargeter noticed, had shaved areas and stitches on the back of their necks, like Nana when Jasmine Angold had first seen her at Bailey Dalrymple's clinic.

In the smaller cage at the back of the minivan, Mrs Pargeter was seated on an upholstered bench seat and chained to the metal rails either side. It struck her that this was probably where the late Doreen Grange had sat on her journeys to and from Atmos, crocheting away at her hideous and variegated PhiliPussies.

The heat inside the vehicle and the Mediterranean landscape visible through the van's windows – not to mention the dire quality of the road they were driving along – suggested they might still be in Greece, though probably by now on the mainland.

Fortunately for Mrs Pargeter, the concentration that he had to put into his driving meant that Costas Philippoussis had not noticed that she had woken up. She narrowed her eyes to slits so that she would still look as though she was unconscious and tried to work out how she could escape her current predicament.

The first good thing was that she wasn't dead. When she'd seen the tartan dog lead as she lost consciousness in the PhiliPussies cat sanctuary on Atmos, part of her had feared that she was about to suffer the same fate as Doreen Grange. But with returning consciousness came the certainty that that was not an immediate danger. Rochelle Brighouse wanted her alive. She wanted her alive to tell all the contacts from the little black book to open up to her son Haydon's questioning. In fact, to persuade them to reveal all the closely guarded secrets of the late Mr Pargeter's business affairs.

There was no way Mrs Pargeter was going to let that happen.

Through the lashes of her half-closed eyes, she continued to assess her situation. She was attached to the bench seat with a broad chain tight around her midriff. Her arms were kept away from her body with cuffs chained to the van's side walls, making it impossible for her to reach anything with them. Her legs had not been chained but, given how firmly her upper body was immobilized, their relative freedom was of little benefit to her.

She looked from her bodily restraints to the next level of her incarceration. She could not see behind her, but the position of the bench seat and its rigidity suggested that her cage was four-sided. No easy access to the van's back doors then.

There was a door in the front of her cage, but that was firmly chained up. Mrs Pargeter didn't mind that. At least it kept her safe from the slashing attentions of the cacophony of cats in the cage in front. That too had a chained door which would open on to the space where the van's passenger seat had been removed. The vehicle had been customized for its PhiliPussies purposes.

Just the one driver, though. Mrs Pargeter had seen no evidence of roads on Atmos, so presumably the cats had been transferred from a boat to the minivan on Skiathos. Or perhaps the change of transport had been achieved at a mainland port.

Mrs Pargeter had been so deeply under the effects of the butorphanol that she had no recollection of how she had arrived in her current plight.

All she knew was that her head ached wickedly, her mouth was drier than ever and her spirits had lost much of their customary bounce. For the time being she could do nothing, and she didn't relish the prospects of what might happen when she was finally released from her incarceration.

Then, as so often happened on those rare occasions when Mrs Pargeter felt low, a new thought came bursting into her mind and irradiated its gloom.

The chains that held her to the chair and the chains that kept the two cages closed were all fastened by padlocks.

There is a lot to be said for having large breasts. Not only do they guarantee a level of masculine attention – which can sometimes become excessive – but a large cleavage can also at times serve as a very useful hiding place. In costume plays what is usually hidden in the bosom is an incriminating love letter, but the objects that Mrs Pargeter had inserted into her brassiere that morning were considerably more practical.

And one of them, of course, was Parvez the Peterman's Padlock Pass.

Unable to use her hands to position the device correctly, Mrs Pargeter had to do a certain amount of jiggling to get it pointing in the right direction. And more jiggling to make sure that she would be putting pressure on the green opening button rather than the red closer. But she could see far enough down into her cleavage to get that right.

Then, once it was safely nuzzled between her breasts, she had to be very careful about the precise direction of its beam. She had to zap the padlocks in the correct order. For example, if she were to release the vicious cats from their cage into hers, the results could be very unpleasant.

So she made certain that the Padlock Pass was pointing directly at the foremost padlock in the minivan. Then she looked out of the vehicle's front windows to see if the terrain was suitable for what she had in mind. They were still driving on a very bad surface, but for the time being the roadsides were too open to suit her plans. It was only when the minivan entered a thickly forested area that she knew her moment had come.

Straining against the chains that held her arms back, she hunched her shoulders forwards so that her breasts were pressing hard on the Padlock Pass between them.

The first time she made the effort, nothing happened. Nor did it the second time. Third time lucky, though.

She heard and felt the click of the green button being pressed, and was instantly rewarded by the snap of the padlock bursting open and the jangle of chains opening the heavy mesh door which separated the cats from the minivan's front cabin.

Yowling victoriously, the feline stormtroopers crowded through the opening.

Suddenly attacked, Costas Philippoussis didn't know what had hit him. Maybe it was just in their feral nature, or maybe they reckoned they had personal scores to settle with their captor, but all of the cats attacked him with razor-sharp teeth and extended claws.

The driver's hands left the wheel as he tried to beat off his assailants. The minivan careered off, out of control, and smashed into a roadside tree. Costas's body was jerked forward and his forehead met the windscreen with a satisfying thwack. He lay still.

Unhurriedly, Mrs Pargeter zapped free the padlocks on the chains that restrained her arms. With her hands free, it was easy to release the chain around her waist, then the one that secured the door of her cage.

She moved gingerly forward, not wishing to make herself another target for the ferocious felines, and slid open the van's side door. The cats, sensing the smells of the outdoors and the freedom they represented, left their prey and rocketed out to enjoy the enticing pleasures of liberty.

Mrs Pargeter inspected Costas Philippoussis and was glad to see that he was still alive. Groans and slight movements suggested he might be coming out of his stupor, so before he became properly awake, she fixed the chains that had restrained her arms on to his wrists and padlocked the other ends to the steering wheel.

She didn't think Costas would come to further harm if she just left him where he was. They had encountered a few other vehicles on the stony roads. Somebody would come along and release him before too long.

Mrs Pargeter picked up her belongings from the well next to the driver's seat. She transferred the invaluable contents of her brassiere back into her handbag.

When she got out of the minivan she could smell the sea and walked towards it. As the trees began to thin out and give way to a beach, she sat down and got out her mobile phone.

She rang HRH back in Berkeley Square. He identified her exact location, on the coast of the Greek mainland just near Thessaloniki.

Within half an hour the helicopter he'd arranged had landed on the beach to pick up Mrs Pargeter and fly her away.

TWENTY-EIGHT

Mrs Pargeter took advantage of HRH's offer of a few hours in a luxury hotel before the private jet waiting at Thessaloniki would take her back to London City Airport. She felt in need of a shower and a change of clothes. Everything she had on smelt of cat.

Once she was clean and resplendent in a turquoise silk dress, she assessed her situation. Though satisfied with the way she had escaped from Costas Philippoussis and the minivan, she was far from relaxed. In fact, she was consumed by anxiety about Truffler Mason.

He was as reliable as the sun rising in the morning. If he said he was going to be somewhere at a given time, he'd be there. So the fact that he hadn't been at Atmos harbour that morning – and the fact that he hadn't contacted her to explain his non-appearance – meant that something unpleasant had happened to him.

Truffler had already antagonized Yannis Philippoussis on his previous visit to Tumblers Tate's cottage. Maybe when he

arrived the second time he'd found a reception committee of
Philippoussis cousins waiting for him. Maybe by the time
Mrs Pargeter encountered them at the harbour, they had already
dealt with Truffler Mason.

She hated to think what form their dealing might take.
Though no members of the Philippoussis clan may have been
directly involved in the murder of Doreen Grange, Mrs Pargeter
felt pretty sure that they knew about it. She also felt that there
had to be some criminal connection between the Greek and
British operations of the PhiliPussies charity. But she couldn't
for the life of her work out what it might be.

She found herself to be extremely frustrated and even a
bit vulnerable. Her first instinct in a situation like this would
have been to ring Truffler. He could always see a way round
practical challenges.

But of course ringing him was the one thing she couldn't do.

She rang Gary instead.

'Hi, Mrs P. How are you? Still sunning yourself on that
Greek island?'

'Hardly sunning myself, and I'm not on the island. But I
am still in Greece. I'll be flying back to London City Airport
later in the day.'

'Tell me when you get in and I'll be there with the Roller
to take you back to Chigwell.'

'No, there's something more urgent you need to do for me,
Gary.'

And she hastily explained what had happened to Truffler
Mason – or rather, she explained why she didn't know what
had happened to Truffler Mason.

'So you reckon he's still on the island?'

'I can't think where else he could be.'

'No.' Gary was thoughtfully silent for a moment. Then he
said, 'Look, I'll get on to HRH to organize transport. I assume
he's sorted yours out?'

'Yes.'

'Of course. Anyway, leave it with me, Mrs P. If Truffler's
still on that island, I'll find him.'

'Well, do be careful. Like I say, all of the Philippoussis
family seem to be unreconstructed thugs.'

Gary sounded affronted. 'I know how to look after myself.'

'I know you do, but I don't think you should come out alone.'

He took this as an affront to his masculinity. 'I can *manage*,' he insisted.

'The thing is,' said Mrs Pargeter diplomatically, 'that I think finding Truffler might require special skills.'

'How'dja mean?'

'The last time I saw Truffler, he was off to visit Tumblers Tate. Now, I don't need to tell you that Tumblers Tate is renowned as the world's most accomplished cracksman.'

'I'd go along with that.'

'Which means it might turn out, Gary, that rescuing Truffler could involve some special cracksman's skills.'

'With you.'

'So I suggest you ask Parvez the Peterman if he'll come with you.'

'Good thinking, Mrs P.'

Shortly after the end of that call, Mrs Pargeter received a text message from HRH to say that Tumblers Tate was dead. No details, just the announcement. She worried what effect the death would have – or had had – on Truffler Mason.

It was early evening when Mrs Pargeter left Thessaloniki Airport in the private jet HRH had organized for her. He also arranged a limousine to meet her flight and take her home to Chigwell.

All very smooth and efficient. But she didn't sleep well that night.

She was too worried about Truffler.

TWENTY-NINE

The following morning Mrs Pargeter had a call from Ellie Fenchurch. 'I've got all the dirt on that conniving specimen of pond life Haydon Brighouse,' she announced.

'Oh, really? What have you found out?'

'Where shall I start? He's a kleptomaniac, did you know that?'

'Yes, I did.'

'And he's the kind of writer who gives journalism a bad name.'

'Oh?'

'He works down the lowest end of the gutter press. And that's where he gets his ideas from – the gutter. No one can have any secrets from people like him. He'll publish any muck he can rake up.'

Mrs Pargeter smiled inwardly. Exactly the same criticisms had frequently been levelled at Ellie herself, though she wouldn't have recognized the description. 'And is he aiming to publish the muck he's raked up about my husband and the . . . I can't remember the name of his supposed rivals . . .?'

'The Lambeth Walkers,' Ellie supplied. 'Oh yes, he's working on that. His deadline's end of the month, three weeks' time.'

'Who's his publisher?'

'Puff Adder Press.'

'I don't know anything about them.'

'You don't want to know anything about them. They're the pits. Everything they publish is lurid, scurrilous rubbish that only appeals to people down the pervy end of the True Crime market.'

'So if Haydon's book has to be delivered by the end of the month, when are they likely to publish it?'

'Puff Adder Press don't hang about. Minimal copy-editing, virtually no fact-checking; they get their books on sale in a couple of months.'

All Mrs Pargeter said was, 'Hm', but that was an inadequate expression of her disquiet. The prospective publication of a book traducing her husband's reputation within three months was almost as worrying as the fate of Truffler Mason.

On the plane out to Skiathos, Gary and Parvez the Peterman studied closely the dossier that HRH had prepared for them. He understood the problems of landing in hostile territory.

They were given details of Demetrios, the man they had to contact who would provide the boat for them on Skiathos and directions to the small cove on Atmos where they could arrive unobserved by the massed Philippoussises.

HRH's service was nothing if not thorough.

'Erin, love,' asked Mrs Pargeter, 'as you know, I'm totally ignorant when it comes to computers . . .'

'No worries,' said the voice from the other end of the line. 'I'm not, so if you have a computer problem, all you have to do is ask me.'

'Yes, thank you. Now I've heard of this thing called "hacking" . . .'

'Mm.'

'Which, as I understand it, involves getting into the data on other people's computers . . .'

'That's right.'

'And I just wondered . . . Have you ever done that, Erin?'

The girl sounded amazed that the question was being asked. 'Of course. Do it all the time. That's how I get most of my information.'

'Oh, good.'

'Why – is there someone whose computer you want me to get into?'

'Yes, there is.' And Mrs Pargeter explained the plan that was beginning to take shape in her mind.

Everything went smoothly on Skiathos. Gary and Parvez the Peterman met the man described in HRH's dossier. Demetrios took them to the very neat small inflatable with a large outboard motor which would be perfect for their purposes. It was moored against the jetty of a tiny cove away from the main drag of the town.

There was a small taverna on the beach. Demetrios said it was too early for them to set off for Atmos – it was important they arrived there after dark – and suggested they had a drink there while they waited.

Both of the visitors drank sparkling water. Parvez the Peterman didn't touch alcohol for religious reasons, and Gary knew – though it'd be in a boat rather than a car – that he had some challenging driving ahead. And once again he was grateful to the late Mr Pargeter, who had ensured his training meant that he could get away just as efficiently on water as he could on land.

About the time that they sat down in the taverna, two hours behind in Chigwell Mrs Pargeter rang through to Jasmine Angold. She gave no signs of the anxiety that still clawed away at her, but asked tenderly about how her friend – and of course her friend's new cat – were doing.

'Oh, Nana and I have bonded completely. We were made for each other. And you know what – in spite of what that vet in Leigh-on-Sea said – Nana's actually pregnant. We're going to have kittens!'

Mrs Pargeter tried to sound appropriately enthusiastic. Then she asked after Charley.

'She's fine.'

'Getting on with the book, is she?'

'Not very well, I'm afraid.'

'Jasmine, I wonder whether it's really a good idea for her to be writing this book . . .'

'She has to,' her friend responded doggedly. 'It was Silver's last wish.'

'Yes, but I—'

'She must do it.' That was a position on which Jasmine Angold was not going to shift.

'I wonder . . . could I have a word with Charley?'

The girl's mother sounded slightly puzzled as she said, 'Yes. Yes, of course you can.'

'It's just . . . I've thought of a little project that might interest her . . .'

As HRH had promised, there was only a small sickle moon that night as Gary and Parvez the Peterman made landfall on Atmos. They dragged their inflatable up on to the shingle. Parvez took out the aluminium suitcase which contained all his working tools, and Gary checked that the automatic pistol was snug in his trouser pocket. Then they consulted the map that HRH had provided and set off, walking silently on the sand, towards the cottage of Tumblers Tate – or now, as they had been informed, of the late Tumblers Tate.

THIRTY

'Charley, I've had a thought about the book that you're supposed to be writing.'

'Really? "Supposed to be" is right. I'm sorry, Mrs Pargeter, but I'm not getting anywhere on it. I'm realizing increasingly that I am just not cut out to write fiction.'

'Does it have to be fiction?'

'What do you mean?'

'I have a non-fiction project that I thought might interest you.'

'Really?' The girl's manner changed instantly from lethargic to intrigued. 'What is it?'

'I wonder . . . would you be able to meet me for lunch at Greene's Hotel tomorrow . . .?'

Following HRH's instructions, Gary and Parvez had no difficulty in locating Tumblers Tate's cottage. The cracksman clicked open his box of tricks to tackle the front door lock, but when Gary pushed, it opened.

Only when they were safely inside did they switch on their torches. Having not seen the place before, they weren't aware of how thoroughly it had been stripped of all Tumblers Tate's possessions. There were almost no signs of human habitation. The Philippoussis cousins might not have decided yet what use they would put the cottage to in the future, or whether they'd just leave it empty.

When their torch beams reached the terrace at the back, they found its furniture had not been moved. The couple of chairs were still there. So was the small table, though only the nearly empty brandy bottle remained on its surface.

And the dilapidated lounger remained in place. Of course

neither Gary nor Parvez the Peterman knew how recently it had been supporting the corpse of Tumblers Tate. But the lounger was unoccupied now. The Philippoussis cousins must have removed the body for funeral and burial – or perhaps some less formal and simpler means of disposal.

The beam of Gary's torch found a familiar beige raincoat folded over the back of a chair. 'Well, Truffler's certainly been here,' he observed.

There was a sniffing noise behind him. He turned to see Parvez the Peterman savouring the air on the terrace as though it were a fine wine.

'My nose tells me,' he said, 'that he might well still be here.'

'Sorry to ring you so late, Erin.'

'No worries, Mrs P. I'm rather a night owl. Do a lot of my best work in the small hours.'

'That's fine then. I was wondering, Erin, whether you might be free tomorrow for lunch at Greene's Hotel . . .?'

'What is it you can smell?' asked Gary.

'Beeswax . . . and a bit of pine rosin.'

'So what does that mean? They probably make candles from beeswax out here. And I could smell the pine trees as we were coming along the beach.'

'No, I'm talking pine *rosin*. It smells slightly different from the actual trees.'

Gary shrugged. 'OK. So how does that help us?'

'Tumblers Tate made up a recipe for a lubricant, you know, to ease locks and jammed cogs and sliding doors. Worked a treat.'

'And . . .?'

'And, because I can smell beeswax and pine rosin here, it suggests to me that he probably built some secret hideaway not far from where we are right now, whose door is greased by the special lubricant that he invented.'

'What – here?' Gary sprayed the beam of his torch around the terrace area. Then he focused it on the uneven paving of the floor. 'Under that lot, do you reckon?'

Parvez the Peterman walked along the area back and forth, his torch pointing downwards, examining every stone and speck of dust. 'No,' he announced finally. 'The surface would be disturbed if anything had been opened here.'

'Where then?' asked Gary. Parvez the Peterman's torch beam strayed towards the sheer rock wall that marked the end of the terrace. 'You gotta be joking. That's solid. No one could make a hideaway in that.'

Parvez raised a finger of dissent. 'Only one person could. And that person's Tumblers Tate.'

'Well, good luck in trying to get in there,' said Gary disconsolately as he slumped in a chair. 'How're you going to do it – rub a magic lamp?'

Parvez the Peterman opened his aluminium case. 'I don't have one of those, but I do have a variety of devices which might have the same effect.'

A contemptuous 'Huh' was all the response he got.

But, in spite of his apparent indifference, Gary watched intrigued as the cracksman focused a series of beams on the wall of rock. These sensors provided him with information which appeared on the screen of his laptop. So far as Gary could tell, Parvez's approach was based on trial and error. Most of his attempts to hack into Tumblers Tate's sophisticated electronic systems were unsuccessful, but every now and then he tested something that seemed to give him satisfaction. Gary was impressed by the patience with which Parvez tried out combination after combination. He seemed to get into a state of Zen concentration and calm.

It was probably a couple of hours later, and the chauffeur, tired out by his rushed journey from London, was quietly dozing, when Parvez the Peterman suddenly announced, 'We're there!'

'Er . . .?' asked Gary blearily.

'I've got through the security system.'

The news brought the chauffeur back to instant consciousness. 'Blimey, well done.'

'Yes.' Parvez's lip curled in frustration. 'We're there, all but for one thing.'

'What's that?'

'His last security barrier, which if I know anything about Tumblers Tate, is going to be something that isn't electronic.'

'How'd'ja mean?'

'I mean it'll be some biometric system. Retinal scanning, iris recognition, fingerprint, maybe even voice activation.'

'I hope it's not the last one,' said Gary. 'Since the old geezer croaked it's going to be kinda hard to get him talking.'

'It's going to be kinda hard to get any of the other biometrical access methods either . . .'

'Yes.'

'. . . unless we can find Tumblers Tate's body.'

Mrs Pargeter went to bed that night, again in little expectation of sleep. She looked fondly at the photograph of her husband, and not for the first time wished he was there to sort things out. He would know how to find and rescue Truffler.

So, though she was feeling pleased about the idea she was going to put to Charley and Erin the following day, she could only look forward to another night of anxiety.

'Where do we find his body?' asked Gary.

'Well, if the Philippoussises have gone down the traditional route, they'll probably have had his funeral already.'

'Oh?'

'They tend to be quick off the mark in hot countries. So he could be buried in a graveyard by now. Might be tricky getting him out of that.'

'I'm sure we could manage,' said Gary, ever the optimist.

'Alternatively, because Tumblers Tate was a crook, and involved in some of the Philippoussises' jobs, they might just have dumped him unceremoniously in the sea, no questions asked.'

Gary's optimism was challenged. 'So where do we start looking for him?'

'We don't start looking for him yet,' said Parvez decisively. 'There's other things to look for first.'

'Like what?'

'The scanning device he used to recognize his retina or his iris or his fingerprint . . . whatever part of his body he used to open and close the place.'

'You seem pretty certain that the hideaway's here.'

'Oh, it is.' Parvez the Peterman gestured to his laptop. 'I've got data on that which shows its precise location and dimensions.' He looked with frustration at the rock face ahead of him. 'I've also detected the warmth of a human body in there. It's got to be Truffler.'

'No possibility we could get a sledgehammer and some crowbars and break into the . . .' The expression on Parvez's face dried up Gary's words at source.

'No, what we've got to do,' said the cracksman, 'is to find that scanner.'

Only a few feet away from them, inside Tumblers Tate's vault, Truffler Mason was no longer photographing anything. The battery on his mobile had long ago run down. And he was starting to feel sleepy again. He'd begun his incarceration by reading a lot of the records of the deceased cracksman's crimes and sleeping a little. Now the balance had changed. A few pages of the files and he'd feel the need to sleep again. His strength, he knew, was waning.

'Got it!' Parvez the Peterman felt under the arm of the lounger and turned it over in triumph. The small electronic pad was revealed. 'Looks like just a thumbprint. We're in luck!'

'Are you sure?' asked Gary. 'You may know it's a thumb-print, but I can't help pointing out we still don't have the thumb required. It's still attached to Tumblers Tate's body and we don't know where that is.'

'A detail,' said Parvez. 'We've got ways round that.'

'Have we?'

'Yes.' He took a pair of goggle-like glasses out of his case and put them on. Then he picked up the empty Courvoisier bottle.

'What're those for?'

'They're for multispectral imaging.'

'Yeah. And what's that when it's at home?'

'It recognizes and highlights individual fingerprints.' Parvez peered closely at the bottle. 'There – perfect. That's a beauty.'

He replaced the bottle on the table and took a small

camera-like device out of his case. A quick click and he was checking some data on the laptop. 'Great. Just print that up.'

He pressed a couple of keys, there was a whirring noise from inside the aluminium box of tricks, and after a moment he pulled out a small rectangle of something that looked like silicone.

He offered it to Gary for inspection. 'See, it's got the contour and ridges of Tumblers Tate's thumbprint – life-size. Not bad, is it?'

'But will it work?'

'Oh yes,' Parvez replied with complete confidence, 'it'll work.'

He pressed the indented false thumbprint against the sensor pad on the underside of the lounger's arm.

Instantly, silently, a section of the rock face moved forward and slid to one side.

In the illuminated interior, Truffler Mason looked out blearily.

'Gary, Parvez,' he said. 'How good of you to come.'

THIRTY-ONE

T ruffler was very weak, but he could stand and, he reckoned, make it to the inflatable with a couple of shoulders to lean on. In the boat, Gary promised, were food and drink for him to start building up his strength again.

They decided they'd close up the cell again when they left. 'There's evidence in there,' said Truffler, 'that could bring down a good few major villains. We don't want the Philippoussises getting their dirty mitts on it.'

Then, just as he was coming out of his prison, Truffler said, 'Ooh, there's something there for you, Parvez.'

'What?'

A long finger was pointed at the letter on the table. Parvez the Peterman looked with surprise at his own name written on the envelope.

He opened it, and read the contents in bewilderment. Then he read them again. As he passed the letter to the other two, a smile was crinkling around the corners of his mouth.

What Gary and Truffler read was:

> *Dear Parvez,*
> *I know it'll be you. You are the only person in the world who has got the skills to break into this place. I'd like to congratulate you on that achievement. And on your many other achievements. You are the only rival I ever worried about. It was always you and me, jockeying for the top spot, with the rest nowhere. And if you've managed to get in here, then I think we're level. If, on the other hand, I am dead by the time you read this letter, then there's no question about it. You, Parvez the Peterman, are undoubtedly the best cracksman in the world. Many, many congratulations!*
> *Tumblers Tate*

The smile crinkling around Parvez's mouth had now developed into a full beam.

The sickle moon gave little light as the three men, Truffler Mason being supported on either side by Gary and Parvez, made their way back to the inflatable. Truffler was too weak to help them drag the boat over the shingle and sand to the sea. But, once it was afloat, they helped him in. Parvez plied him with dried apricots, brandy and mineral water, while Gary started up the outboard motor.

'Skiathos, here we come!' he murmured.

It was as they passed the harbour mouth that they became aware they were being followed. Floodlight beams were suddenly switched on in the boat that roared out after them. They could see the flashes and hear the whine of gunshots, never the most encouraging form of attack for people in an inflatable.

The lights blinded them, so they couldn't see who was in the other vessel, but from everything they had heard they knew it must be full of Philippoussis cousins.

'Hold on tight!' Gary shrieked as he swung the boat round on its axis to evade the flying bullets.

He looked out towards the open sea, beyond the line of rocks that formed one arm of Atmos harbour. Out there they would stand no chance. The Philippoussis cousins' more powerful vessel would overtake and cut them down in no time.

'Any ideas, Truffler?' he shouted against the roar of the engines. 'You've had time to get to know the place a bit.'

'Yes,' the rescued man said calmly. 'Aim straight for the rocks.'

Gary had known and trusted Truffler too long to argue. He swung the tiller on the outboard again, through nearly three hundred and sixty degrees. His passengers were hurled against the boat's sides, as he followed instructions and made a course straight for the rocks.

The larger vessel couldn't manoeuvre as quickly as the inflatable, but it was soon once again following them, gaining with every second. Bullets continued to hiss around them.

'There!' Truffler Mason's finger jabbed forward, and for the first time Gary saw thin moonlight reflecting on the sea beyond the rocks. There was a gap in them. Twisting the throttle to screeching point, he made for that gap.

It was the Widowmaker. Narrow. Too narrow even for the inflatable, it seemed, as they hurtled towards it. But still Gary did what Truffler told him, even though he could envisage how the rocky sides of the archway would shred the rubber of their boat.

Just as that moment seemed unavoidable, Truffler shouted, 'Move your bodies to the right!'

The three men did as instructed. The inflatable tipped at an angle, its outboard motor shrieking complaint at being out of the water, and slid through the narrow passage. Within seconds they were on the calm, flat, open sea beyond.

The chasing vessel was not so lucky. Travelling too fast to be stopped, its sides jammed in the Widowmaker's jaws. There was a splintering of timbers and a shattering of glass.

Fortunately, no widows were made that night, but a lot of Philippoussis cousins did get extremely wet.

*   *   *

In the open sea beyond, Gary cut back the power of the outboard and the inflatable chugged contentedly back towards Skiathos.

Truffler grinned across at him. 'Glad to see the old getaway driving instincts are still in full working order, Gary.'

'Mr Pargeter taught me well,' came the reply.

Truffler's mobile was out of power, but he borrowed Parvez the Peterman's to text Mrs Pargeter and tell her he was absolutely fine.

THIRTY-TWO

Mrs Pargeter felt more cheerful than ever as one of Gary's drivers helped her out of the Rolls-Royce at Greene's Hotel soon after noon on the following day. The news of Truffler's release had come as a wonderful relief at one o'clock in the morning, and made her realize how much she cared for him. Once she had recovered from her excitement, she slipped into the blissful sleep she had been deprived of over the previous two nights, and didn't wake till after ten. Gary's driver even had to wait while she bathed and dressed.

On the way into London she made one phone call. To someone who appeared in the currently inaccessible little black book. It was listed, she remembered, under 'Explosive Experts' and he was called 'Jelly Jones'. Fortunately, she remembered being told his real name by Truffler. He also told her that he had become a Professor of Chemistry at University College, London. So that was the number she rang.

When Jelly Jones heard who was on the line he was fulsomely delighted to interrupt the lecture he was giving and talk to her. It was such an honour, he'd been so privileged to work with the late Mr Pargeter, who had been one of the finest men on God's earth, etc., etc., etc.

Mrs Pargeter managed to break into this familiar litany to tell Jelly Jones the reason for her call. He would, of course, be delighted to be of service to her, and they fixed to meet at UCL at three thirty that afternoon.

Hedgeclipper Clinton was, as ever, enchanted to welcome his most honoured guest into his palace of a hotel. He personally escorted her to the private room she had booked for her lunch *à trois*. In anticipation of her next request, a newly opened bottle of champagne stood in the ice bucket. Hedgeclipper poured a glass for Mrs Pargeter and left her to await her guests.

She sipped the champagne as she planned what her next moves should be. The news about Truffler had lifted her mood of frustration and she felt more positive than ever. Things, she had a sense, were coming to a head. She had almost all the information she required to turn the tables on Rochelle Brighouse and to remove the threat posed by her son's forthcoming book. It was just a matter of taking the right steps in the right order.

Her phone blipped to alert her to an incoming text message. It was sent from Parvez the Peterman's phone, though the message wasn't from him.

Just changing planes at Paris Charles de Gaulle. Be at Heathrow in less than an hour. As soon as I've charged my mobile, I will be forwarding you a very interesting set of documents.

Let us know what you want us to do and where you want us to be when. We'll be there. All the best, Truffler.

That made her feel even better. For the plan that was forming in her head, she might well be glad of a protective escort.

And when copies of the documents Truffler had photographed came through on her phone and she read them, her mood bordered on the ecstatic.

Charley and Erin arrived at the same time. They had met in the lift and bonded instantly. They were already chattering away as the waiter poured champagne for them.

After their starters had been served, Mrs Pargeter outlined what she wanted them both to do. 'For you, Erin, it will involve hacking into someone's computer and replacing the data in there with something new.'

'No probs. As I told you, that's what I spend most of my time doing.'

'And for you, Charley . . .'

'You said it was something to do with writing a non-fiction book.'

'Yes.'

'About what?'

'Charley, I want you to write a memoir of my late husband.'

The lunch was an extremely jolly affair. The Greene's Hotel food was as exquisite as ever. Mrs Pargeter spelled out the details of her plans, and the two girls were delighted with the tasks assigned to them. Once that had all been sorted, the conversation became more general. Without the subject ever being mentioned, Mrs Pargeter was aware how her two guests were bonded by both having relatively recently lost their fathers.

So jolly was the lunch that when the second bottle of champagne had been finished and the third one ordered, Mrs Pargeter found to her amazement that it was nearly a quarter to three. She must leave for her appointment with Jelly Jones.

She proposed that the girls should stay and finish the new bottle, a suggestion to which they readily agreed.

By the time she got down to the foyer, Hedgeclipper Clinton had seen to it that the Rolls-Royce with Gary's driver inside was waiting directly outside the main doors.

Mrs Pargeter asked to be taken to UCL.

Her meeting with Jelly Jones was extremely successful. He confirmed that what she suspected was true.

The driver took her back to Chigwell and, once in the house, Mrs Pargeter made a call to Bailey Dalrymple. At the start of the conversation he was as bonhomous as ever, but after she'd told him what she knew, his manner was markedly less relaxed.

But he did agree that they should meet. That evening, yes, the sooner the better. And no, not at the PhiliPussies clinic in Leigh-on-Sea. Too much danger of being heard there.

Instead he proposed that they should meet at eight o'clock in Epping Forest. Near the place where Doreen Grange's body had been found. (Bailey didn't actually say that, but from his directions for getting there, Mrs Pargeter recognized where it was.)

Mrs Pargeter knew it was a trap. But she felt confident of her own safety now Truffler and Gary were back in the country. She texted to Truffler's phone, giving exact directions for where she, Gary and Truffler should meet at seven thirty that evening.

There were a few hours before she'd need to be driven to Epping Forest. She'd recommended that Gary's driver should pick her up in something less flamboyant than the Roller – though she actually reckoned there was a good chance that Gary himself would drive her.

Full of her lavish Greene's Hotel lunch, and still with sleep to catch up on after her two bad nights, Mrs Pargeter lay on the sofa in her sitting room and drifted into blameless unconsciousness.

And, as she did so, her last thought was that things were definitely coming to a head.

THIRTY-THREE

With Mrs Pargeter gone, the two girls in the private room at Greene's Hotel had first got on to the subject of boyfriends. Neither had had particularly fruitful experiences in that area, so they had an agreeable moan together about the inadequacies of the male of the species.

And then, inevitably, they did actually start to talk about their fathers. Charley was envious of the bonding over the archives that Erin and Jukebox Jarvis had shared during his last six months. She wished she'd had as much quality time together with 'Silver' Angold.

'I agree. I was lucky,' said Erin, 'and working with Dad on

all those records did kind of clarify things for me, you know, what I wanted to do with my life. It made me realize that my real aim was to spend the rest of my life doing what my father had done – except of course with all the advantages that modern technology can bring to the work.'

'Did your father make demands on you, Erin? You know, tell you how he wanted you to use the archive after he was gone?'

'Not really. That had all been sorted out during the time that we were updating it.'

'Again you were lucky.' Charley sighed. 'No postmortem demands.'

'Are you suggesting that your father did make demands on you, that he's still making demands on you from beyond the grave?'

'And how!' So Charley Angold explained to Erin about the letter her father had left for her – and the burden it had imposed. 'The trouble is,' she concluded, 'that my mother's absolutely insistent that I should obey my father's dying wish. And get a bloody book published.'

'Well, at least what Mrs Pargeter was talking about today does show you a way of doing it.'

'Oh yes, bless her. I was going mad trying to write a novel. The stories I wrote at school may have showed promise, but my brain just doesn't work that way any more. Now, thank the Lord, Mrs Pargeter has shown me an escape route.'

'She's very clever,' said Erin, and Charley nodded agreement.

There was a silence. They sipped their champagne. Then Erin said, 'This letter your father left you . . . do you have it with you?'

'Not the original – that's at home. But I do have a photocopy.'

'Would you mind awfully if I had a look at it?'

'Not at all.' Charley was already rooting through her handbag. 'Can I ask you why, though?'

''Course you can. It just sounds a bit odd. And, as someone who likes doing crosswords, I have an instinct to examine anything that sounds odd to see if it has another meaning.'

'My father liked crosswords too – tried to get me interested, but I just don't think I've got that kind of brain.' Charley handed across the much-perused photocopy. 'Anyway,' she said, 'if you can find another meaning in that – a meaning that means I don't have to publish any kind of bloody book – I will be more than grateful to you.'

'Let's have a look . . .' Erin spread the sheet of paper on the tablecloth and read it through.

Dear Charley,
Might your old father give you a word of advice?
Might your old father point you in a useful direction?
Ask who always loved you from when you were a tiny baby?
The champion who stood up for you against everyone?
Only me.
You stirred in me emotions I did not know I had.
I did not expect to feel such total love,
Such a subtle change in my personality
From a rough, uncaring man to a helpless father,
Hopelessly enthralled by this perfect person
Whose tiny life had suddenly become so important to me.
So know my love is there forever,
Whether I live a reasonably long time or die young.
But there's a last thing I want you to do for me,
Do not think me terrible to ask this . . .
But I always felt pleased when you did well at English.
So, for me, your old Dad, please write a book,
Get it published, into major bookstores
And other outlets, even e-books if you must,
So long as it is out there existing for the general public to read,
You will know for sure that you have done the right thing by your poor old Dad
And I will be able to rest easy wherever it is I end up.
What kind of book you write . . . it doesn't matter to me,
So long as the thing is published in some form or other,
Be it hardback, paperback or presentation copy.
I know you may find it's hard but, if you ever loved me,

Do as this letter tells you and lo – all your wishes for
*   future prosperity*
For you and for your mother should instantly come
*   true.*
Follow my instructions – into your writing
Go line by line and progress letter by letter
Until you at last attain the moment of publication.
Then my vast fortune will be yours – and Jasmine
Will benefit too from that vast, vast fortune.
My blessings always will support you both.

There was a long silence before Erin announced, 'Well, there's something very strange with the layout.'

'Yes, I thought that.'

'It's laid out more like a poem than anything else.'

'Well, if it is a poem, it's a bloody awful poem,' said Charley.

'Did your father like poetry?'

'God, no. I never heard him mention a poem during my entire lifetime.'

'Then why's he laid this out like one . . .?' Erin mused.

'I've no idea. I tell you, I've looked at the thing till it's nearly driven me mad and I still can't see any "other meaning" in it.'

'Mm.' Erin's mounting interest showed in the sparkle in her eyes. 'I think there are instructions in here.'

'Instructions?'

'Yes, look at these lines.' She pointed to a few towards the end.

Do as this letter tells you and lo –

'Was your father the kind of man who said, "and lo—"?'

'Certainly not.'

'No, I didn't think he would.' Erin pointed back to the lines.

. . . all your wishes for future prosperity
For you and for your mother should instantly come true.
Follow my instructions.

'"Follow my instructions" – Charley, he's trying to tell you something.'

'Yes, but what?'

'There's got to be a solution in here.' Erin's brow wrinkled with concentration as she read out: "*Go line by line and progress letter by letter*" — that's got to mean something.'

'What, though?' Charley almost screamed with frustration. Erin was seeing the letter for the first time. Charley had spent hours a day since her father's death asking herself these same questions and coming up with no answers.

'Ah,' said Erin. 'Ah, yes. I've got it.'

'Tell me, for God's sake. What have you got?'

"*Go line by line and progress letter by letter*",' Erin repeated. 'That's what you have to do, literally that. "Go line by line and progress letter by letter." See?'

Charley was too disheartened to say anything. She just shook her head.

'Do you mind if I write on this?'

'No. As I say, it's only a photocopy. Do what you want with it.'

'Right.' Erin took a pen out of her handbag and started underlining letters on the page. 'Line by line,' she said, 'and letter by letter . . . So that would mean . . . the first letter on the first line, the second letter on the second line, the third on the third, and so on.'

Her pen moved swiftly until the complete message was spelled out.

D̲ear Charley,
Mi̲ght your old father give you a word of advice?
Mig̲ht your old father point you in a useful direction?
Ask w̲ho always loved you from when you were a tiny baby?
The ch̲ampion who stood up for you against everyone?
Only me̲.
You stir̲red in me emotions I did not know I had.
I did not e̲xpect to feel such total love,
Such a subt̲le change in my personality
From a roug̲h, uncaring man to a helpless father,
Hopelessly e̲nthralled by this perfect person

Whose tiny life had suddenly become so important to me.
So know my love is there forever,
Whether I live a reasonably long time or die young.
But there's a last thing I want you to do for me,
Do not think me terrible to ask this . . .
But I always felt pleased when you did well at English.
So, for me, your old Dad, please write a book,
Get it published, into major bookstores
And other outlets, even e-books if you must,
So long as it is out there existing for the general public
   to read,
You will know for sure that you have done the right thing
   by your poor old Dad
And I will be able to rest easy wherever it is I end up.
What kind of book you write . . . it doesn't matter
   to me,
So long as the thing is published in some form or other,
Be it hardback, paperback or presentation copy.
I know you may find it's hard but, if you ever loved me,
Do as this letter tells you and lo – all your wishes for
   future prosperity
For you and for your mother should instantly come
   true.
Follow my instructions – into your writing
Go line by line and progress letter by letter
Until you at last attain the moment of publication.
Then my vast fortune will be yours – and Jasmine
Will benefit too from that vast, vast fortune.
My blessings always will support you both.

The two girls read out the encoded message together: "'Dig where the fir tree meets the Fairy Path.'"

Erin looked across to Charley and grinned in triumph. 'Does the expression "the Fairy Path" mean anything to you?'

Charley grinned back. 'Oh yes,' she said. 'Oh yes, Erin, it certainly does!'

THIRTY-FOUR

It wasn't Gary himself who picked her up. It was the same driver who'd taken her to Greene's Hotel and back. The car was an unobtrusive Skoda Octavia.

Once she was comfortably installed in the back, he asked if she'd like to listen to the radio, catch up on the news perhaps . . .?

Mrs Pargeter said no, she'd rather travel in silence.

As a result, she did not hear that Heathrow Airport had been closed due to a terrorist alert. Nor could Truffler Mason, Gary and Parvez the Peterman get a message to her that their flight had been stuck on the tarmac at Charles de Gaulle for four hours and was now being diverted to Manchester.

Once arrived in the car park, Mrs Pargeter told the driver not to wait. Gary would be arriving soon and he'd drive her back to Chigwell once her business had been concluded. The June evening was still quite light. Her tryst was scheduled to take place not far from the forest edge. She walked boldly forward, longing to be reunited with Truffler and Gary.

When she arrived at the designated clearing, it was empty. She checked her watch. Twenty past seven. She sat down on a rustic bench, confident that her bodyguards would be there within ten minutes. Truffler and Gary had always been very punctilious about punctuality.

'Well, Mrs Pargeter, you've arrived in good time,' said a cultured voice as Bailey Dalrymple stepped out from behind a thick-trunked fir tree. 'Not to say rather early.'

'Perhaps I couldn't wait to see you . . .?' she suggested, keeping the conversation deliberately light.

The vet also played it cool, flopping casually down on the bench beside her and saying, 'I found it interesting, our conversation on the phone this afternoon.'

'Well, I thought it was probably time for a few home truths.'

'That may have been a rather rash assumption, Mrs Pargeter. Particularly since what you describe as "home truths" are a pack of lies.'

'Ah, if only I could believe that, Bailey. I do have evidence to back up my claims. I have seen both ends of the PhiliPussies operation, both in Leigh-on-Sea and on Atmos.'

'But your allegations would never stand up in court.'

'Oh, I think they would, Bailey. I do have extremely good lawyers. My late husband always insisted that we should have the very best lawyers.'

'If you do have any doubts about the integrity of PhiliPussies, I think you would do well to address them to Mendy Farstairs.'

'I don't believe that'd do a lot of good. Mendy is totally unaware that there is anything wrong with her precious charity.'

'And might not that be because there is nothing wrong with it?'

'How nice it would be to think that, Bailey. Unfortunately, though, such an interpretation doesn't tie in with the facts.'

'Oh?'

'It's been fortunate for you that the old days of quarantine have gone, that cats can be transported from Greece to the United Kingdom without any hassle.'

Mrs Pargeter was really just talking for the sake of talking. She sneaked a look at her watch. Just before seven thirty. Truffler and Gary would be appearing any moment. She looked through the deepening gloom of the forest for any signs of them.

'It has been convenient,' Bailey Dalrymple agreed. 'Keeping the animals in quarantine would just have added another complication to the challenging work done by our charity.'

'And of course, while they were in quarantine, they might have undergone rather closer inspection than they now do when they travel from Atmos to Leigh-on-Sea.'

'What are you saying, Mrs Pargeter?'

'I am saying that, if the cats were examined more closely, the details of your smuggling operation might very soon become public knowledge.'

'"Smuggling operation"?'

'Yes, Bailey. When I came with my friend to see you at

your clinic, I thought what you said about the clumsiness of Greek vets over microchipping was a bit dubious. But I now know why the cats from Atmos all have scars and stitches on the backs of their necks. Quite clever, really – because no customs officer is going to look too closely at a cat that was feral in the first place and has been made even more vicious by being caged in a hot minivan for days on end.'

'I don't know what you're talking about.'

'Oh, you do, Bailey, you do.' Mrs Pargeter reached into her handbag and produced one of the small pellets that she had found in the surgery of the Atmos cat sanctuary, the pellets Jelly Jones had identified for her so readily at UCL that afternoon. 'You know what this is?'

He didn't even bother to protest his ignorance this time, so Mrs Pargeter went on, 'Enriched uranium. Used legitimately in nuclear fuel processors, but not available for purchase by the average citizen. Of considerable value on the black market, though. There are a surprising number of aspiring terrorists who dream of making a dirty bomb. Not that it would cause anything like the same devastation as a proper nuclear device, but it would spread fear and anxiety. And, so far, the UK authorities haven't caught on to the idea of enriched uranium pellets being smuggled into the country inside feral cats from Greece.'

There was a silence, then Bailey Dalrymple asked softly, 'Do you know how Doreen Grange died?'

'I'm pretty sure she was drugged with butorphanol at her sister's house, and probably strangled there. Then brought here for burial.'

'And who do you think killed her?'

'If she'd been killed out on Atmos, I would have had no doubt that Costas Philippoussis had done it. But since she was killed here, I'm afraid I have you in the frame for that particular crime, Bailey.'

'Why?'

'Couple of reasons. For a start, as a vet, you have access to the butorphanol. Then again, you'd do anything Rochelle Brighouse tells you to do.'

'What makes you think that?'

'Because old habits die hard. Because you would have done anything her husband might have told you to do back when you were working for the Lambeth Walkers.' She was quoting from the volumes of information that Truffler Mason had emailed her.

'Hm. You have done your research, Mrs Pargeter.'

'Not all my own efforts. I have had help from other investigators,' she said, thinking again of the sterling work Truffler Mason had done in Tumblers Tate's archive.

'Hm.' Bailey Dalrymple's voice was silky smooth as he asked, 'And do you know *why* Doreen Grange was killed?'

'I assume it was because she had found out information about the smuggling racket that you and Costas Philippoussis were running.'

'Yes, that was the reason. But she hadn't got nearly as much information about it as you have. So if Doreen had to die for the little that she knew, there is even more reason why, I'm afraid, Mrs Pargeter, you too have reached your last moment on earth! And sorry, with you I haven't got time for the butorphanol!'

Bailey Dalrymple moved very quickly. First his left hand snapped out to grab at her throat, while his right reached for something in the pocket of his tweed jacket.

She recognized the tartan as she felt the lead tighten around her neck.

THIRTY-FIVE

It was after seven when the flight from Charles de Gaulle airport containing Truffler Mason, Gary and Parvez the Peterman finally landed at Manchester. And for security reasons there was another half-hour delay before the passengers were allowed off the plane and could finally use their mobile phones.

Truffler immediately found the text from Mrs Pargeter. His long face turned pale as he said, 'Oh my God.'

*   *   *

'Truffler!' Mrs Pargeter tried to shout the name, but the constriction on her neck only allowed a gasp to emerge. And, anyway, no one was there to answer her summons. Truffler Mason was many miles away.

She struggled, but Bailey Dalrymple was far too strong for her. The pain in her neck gave way to a kind of swimming sensation, as consciousness ebbed away.

Then suddenly a jolt ran through the vet's body and the hands tightening the lead dropped away. Mrs Pargeter heard the heavy thump of him falling off the bench on to the forest floor.

She looked up blearily to see the grinning face of Erin Jarvis. Behind her stood Charley Angold. In Erin's hands was the spade with which she had clearly just hit Bailey Dalrymple on the head.

Erin fetched a bottle of water from her car, and swallowing some down made Mrs Pargeter feel better. Her neck was badly bruised and painful, but she would survive.

Erin also brought some rope which she always kept in her car boot – you never knew when you might need some. And with it she expertly tied the still-unconscious Bailey Dalrymple to the bench so that he would not be able to move until the police arrived to arrest him for the attempted murder of Mrs Pargeter, the actual murder of Doreen Grange – and who-knew-what other crimes.

Charley suggested calling the police straight away, but Mrs Pargeter demurred. True to her principle of being as helpful as possible to the constabulary at all times but spending the minimum amount of time in their presence, she would prefer that the police should be alerted just as she and the girls were leaving, so that when they arrived the trussed-up Bailey Dalrymple would be the only human presence in the clearing. Explanations could come later.

For the first time she noticed that Erin wasn't the only one with a spade. Charley was carrying one too. 'What's all this about then?' She chuckled painfully. 'Are you on Bailey Dalrymple's side? Did he delegate you two to dig the shallow grave I was meant to be put in?'

The girls hastened to assure her that that was not the case. And Charley explained about Erin's unlocking of the puzzle contained in her father's farewell letter.

'Oh, that's wonderful!' said Mrs Pargeter. 'I knew there was something odd about the way he'd written that. So you think it was like a treasure map? Instructions about how to find his stash?'

'Exactly that,' said Charley excitedly.

'So that's why you're here?'

'Yes.'

'Well, what's stopping you? Get digging!'

It didn't take long. Charley's memories of walking the 'Fairy Path' while her father invented stories were very vivid, and she knew exactly where he would have hidden anything. 'There was this little patch by the fir tree, which he used to call the "Fairy Circle". He told me that's where all the fairies in Epping Forest used to come to at midnight and dance around until the dawn. That's where we must dig.'

The Fairy Circle was grassed over and showed no signs of digging, but then who knew how long ago 'Silver' Angold had made his deposit in the Bank of Epping Forest?

Charley's intuition proved correct. The two girls had been digging less than a minute before Erin's spade hit something metallic. More soil was removed to reveal the top of a large toolbox, made of some metal that did not corrode or rust.

A bit more digging around the sides and the two girls lifted it free from the ground. Though covered with earth and dust, the toolbox looked remarkably robust.

Its lid was closed with a padlock. 'Oh,' said Erin. 'I haven't got the right tools here to deal with that. Maybe we'd better get it back to your place, Charley, and—'

'No need,' said Mrs Pargeter magisterially. She extracted Parvez the Peterman's Padlock Pass from her handbag, pointed it at the toolbox, pressed the green button and the padlock sprang open.

'Wow! That's a nice bit of kit,' said Erin.

'Very useful,' Mrs Pargeter agreed and then, giving honour where honour was due, told the girls who had invented it.

Both of them looked down at the box. 'Go on, you open it, Charley,' said Erin. 'It's your stuff. He was your dad, after all.'

Mrs Pargeter and Erin were transfixed as Charley slowly raised the lid.

Inside, not in bags or in any other kind of packaging, was a jumble of jewellery which filled the toolbox right to the top.

True to Charley's father's nickname, 'Silver' Angold, there was lots of silver and gold.

Mrs Pargeter smiled. Now there'd be no need for her to intervene in improving Jasmine Angold's financial situation.

THIRTY-SIX

Mrs Pargeter was still in the clearing when she received a call from a very panic-stricken and apologetic Truffler Mason. He explained about the Heathrow closure and diversion to Manchester.

'No worries,' Mrs Pargeter croaked. 'All in hand. I'm a bit tired now, but I'll ring you in the morning and explain everything.'

Erin and Charley asked her advice about when to alert the police to the presence of Bailey Dalrymple, still unconscious, tied to a bench in Epping Forest.

'What I suggest you do,' she replied, 'is to take Silver Angold's stash back to your place, Charley. Then you drive home, Erin, and call the police from there.'

'Why,' asked Charley, 'can't I call them?'

'Because,' Mrs Pargeter explained, 'until you and your mum have found the right place to hide that toolbox, you don't want the police snooping around your house, do you?'

'Good point.'

'And, Erin, it might be simpler if you say you were the only witness to Bailey Dalrymple's attack on me.'

'Why's that?'

'Again, to keep them from snooping around Jasmine and Charley.'

'Gotcha. Do you think my testimony will be enough to get him convicted?'

'Probably. If you have any problems, though, Truffler's got lots of evidence he copied from Tumblers Tate's archive, which show that Bailey Dalrymple was involved in the uranium pellet smuggling right up to his neck.'

Both girls looked at Mrs Pargeter in amazement. 'Who's Tumblers Tate?' asked Charley. 'And what's all this stuff about uranium pellets?'

'I haven't got enough voice to explain now, but rest assured I will fill you in on everything as soon as I can. Now should I ring Gary's car hire service to get me home?'

'Don't worry about that,' said Erin. 'I'll take you. It's virtually on the way.'

When Mrs Pargeter got back to Chigwell, she was too exhausted to do anything other than drink a lot of whisky and ice to anaesthetize her throat and fall into bed. She had a very good night.

But of course when she woke up the next morning, she knew that the case was far from over.

Rochelle and Haydon Brighouse were still both out there, and they weren't about to take what had happened to Bailey Dalrymple lying down. There was a strong chance that they knew she'd found out about the uranium pellet smuggling. She was very far from being out of danger. The villains using Mendy Farstairs' PhiliPussies charity as a front had committed murder at least once and, as Bailey Dalrymple's actions the night before had revealed, would have no compunction about doing it again. And she was their prime target.

But she didn't let a little thing like that change her plans for the day. She had woken with a very sore throat, but otherwise fine. As promised, she rang Truffler Mason, now safely back in the Mason de Vere Detective Agency office, and brought him up to speed with recent events.

He very quickly recognized the danger she was in. 'I'm

going to come over to the house straight away. I can't forgive myself for not being there last night when you needed me.'

'Truffler, you aren't personally responsible for things like terrorist threats to Heathrow Airport.'

'I should have seen a way round it,' he persisted doggedly. His guilt, his feeling that he had let down the late Mr Pargeter by his absence at a moment of danger to his former boss's widow, was not easily assuaged. 'Anyway, you sit tight. I'll be with you in as long as it takes.'

'There's no need to—'

'There's a very definite need to! I'm not going to let you out of my sight, Mrs P, until this whole PhiliPussies business is sorted.'

When the phone call was finished, Mrs Pargeter did feel comforted. Truffler was safe and Truffler was going to look after her. She looked across with gratitude to the photograph of her late husband. Not for the first time, she felt very grateful for the system of protection that he had set up for her.

Then she put the kettle on to make coffee and awaited Truffler's arrival.

Later that day Mrs Pargeter received the first of the expected contacts from Rochelle Brighouse. It came in the form of an email.

I think for the time being, Melita, we have reached an impasse. Bailey Dalrymple may well be tried for murder and attempted murder, but there's no way he's going to implicate me. I have made clear the danger to his wife and children if he so much as mentions my name. So I'll be in the clear there.

I believe you have documents supplied to Truffler Mason by Tumblers Tate, which might cause trouble for me if they were shown to the police, but I don't think you're going to show them to the police. Those documents concern the activities of the Lambeth Walkers, particularly in relation to their rivalry with your husband's operations. If they are made public, they're at least as big a threat to my brother's reputation as they are to me.

So, as I say, we're at an impasse . . . at least until Haydon's book is published. That will really set the cat among the pigeons and – wilfully to mix metaphors – we will then enter a whole new ball game.

Your affectionate sister-in-law,

Rochelle

Mrs Pargeter was not amused by the sarcastic ending to the email. She could also recognize that some of what Rochelle said was true. The only way she could expose her sister-in-law to criminal investigation did run the risk of making public a series of scurrilous lies about the business activities of her late husband. And, though she was completely confident that he had never once broken the law, proving that could be a long and tiresome process. A rather public process, too.

The only comfort she found in the email was the fact that Rochelle had referred to Tumblers Tate 'supplying' Truffler Mason with documents. That meant she did not know about the secret archive behind the cottage on Atmos.

Otherwise, though, Rochelle was right. They were at a kind of impasse.

And the publication of Haydon Brighouse's book did pose a serious threat.

How fortunate that she had worked out a way of nullifying that threat.

Mrs Pargeter set up a series of sessions with Charley Angold. The girl came to Chigwell every morning and interviewed her, recording their conversations on her iPhone. Then in the afternoons she went back to her mother's house in Romford and wrote up Mrs Pargeter's account. Her interviewee was very pleased with the way the project was shaping up, and Charley assured her that the deadline would be met. Though the decoding of her late father's letter meant that she was no longer under any obligation to produce a book, her mother still thought she should "just in case that's what Silver meant", which suited Mrs Pargeter's plans very well.

*   *   *

Meanwhile Erin Jarvis, having successfully hacked into Haydon Brighouse's computer, monitored all his documents and emails.

Just before the end of the month, Charley announced that she had completed her task and, as agreed, she and Mrs Pargeter went to Erin's house to add the final touches to the operation.

Mrs Pargeter had read through Charley's completed manuscript and thought it was excellent. From their interviews the girl had really captured the essence of the late Mr Pargeter. His honesty and generosity shone from her words. Mrs Pargeter's fond recollections of the happiness of their marriage also came across with charm and clarity. And the extent of his philanthropy, about which he had modestly kept quiet during his lifetime, was staggeringly impressive.

Erin supplied them with coffee and Mrs Pargeter was touched with how at ease the two girls were with each other. If nothing else, one very good friendship was going to come out of the case.

But Mrs Pargeter, ever the optimist, was hoping for a lot, lot more.

'Right,' said Erin, 'I've loaded Charley's book on to my laptop. Now all we need to do is put my Remote Deletion programme to work.'

'And you're sure you've got the timing right?'

'Absolutely. I've been checking his emails. Haydon was in touch with Puff Adder Press this morning. He told his editor he's finished tweaking the manuscript. He's got a lunch meeting, then as soon as he gets back home, he'll email the complete book over.'

'Splendid,' said Mrs Pargeter. 'I'm longing to see your Remote Deletion programme in action.'

'I'm afraid there's not much to see. Like most software it all happens inside the computer. But have a look at this. I'm now inside Haydon's laptop.'

Mrs Pargeter and Charley moved to crane over Erin's shoulders and see what was happening.

'Into his documents . . .' the girl went on '. . . and there's the file called "Lambeth Walkers/Mr Pargeter". That's his manuscript, which as you see he last worked on at 11.43 this morning. So . . .' she keyed in some code '. . . I delete that.'

As she spoke the file name disappeared from the screen. 'Then . . .' Erin went on, tapping more keys '. . . I remove all his back-ups.'

'And that even deletes the ones on his memory sticks and the cloud?' asked Charley.

'It certainly does,' replied Erin, with a note of triumph in her voice. 'That particular file of Haydon Brighouse's no longer exists anywhere in the world. Then all I have to do is summon up Charley's manuscript . . . which I have already thoughtfully renamed "Lambeth Walkers/Mr Pargeter" . . . and . . .' she matched her actions to the words '. . . drag it across into Haydon's directory to replace his version of events.'

She grinned at her two admiring spectators. 'All done,' she said.

They only had to wait till the next day. Then a still triumphant Erin Jarvis rang Mrs Pargeter to say that Puff Adder Press had rejected Haydon Brighouse's book. She quoted from the email, '. . . not at all what we were expecting from you. What you have written is far too bland to be of interest to the true crime enthusiast. If I'd wanted you to write a hagiography of the late Mr Pargeter, I would have told you to do so. The second half of your advance, due on delivery of the manuscript, will not be paid, and I can state quite categorically that we will never work together again.'

Two days later Mrs Pargeter read in the *Daily Mail* that a man called Haydon Brighouse had been arrested for the theft of jewellery from the Cartier Boutique in Old Bond Street.

She was unsurprised to receive a call later in the day from Rochelle Brighouse, who wanted to meet. Mrs Pargeter suggested dinner that evening at Greene's Hotel.

Her ever-attendant minder, Truffler Mason, insisted on accompanying her, even to such safe territory as Greene's. But Mrs Pargeter, in her turn, insisted that her dinner with Rochelle should be *tête-à-tête*.

*   *   *

The politeness between the two women was reminiscent of a Cold War summit. 'I was sorry to hear about Haydon,' said Mrs Pargeter.

'Yes. His kleptomania reasserted itself,' Rochelle admitted. 'It's always the case, when he hasn't got a project. It's an illness,' she said defiantly. 'My lawyers will try to get him off on medical grounds.'

'Good luck,' said Mrs Pargeter. 'You said your son hadn't got a project . . .?'

'He had some bad luck with something he was working on – his latest book was rejected.'

'I'm sorry to hear that,' said Mrs Pargeter.

Her sister-in-law looked at her beadily. 'Really? I wouldn't be surprised to find out that you had something to do with that.'

'Me? With Haydon's book being rejected? How could I possibly—?'

'I reckon you have something to do with everything that spoils my plans,' came the venomous response.

'You flatter me,' said Mrs Pargeter. 'I'm just a widow woman, doing a bit of charity work from time to time – there's nothing more to me than that.'

'Huh.'

'Incidentally, talking of charity, are you still involved with PhiliPussies?'

'Oh, haven't you heard – PhiliPussies has been closed down.'

'Really?'

'There's a threat of an investigation by the Charity Commission. Anyway, with the director of its UK operation being on remand on a murder charge . . .'

'Really?' Mrs Pargeter said again. Then she couldn't resist a small, harmless lie. 'I didn't know that.'

Rochelle's only response was another 'Huh.'

'Mendy Farstairs will be very upset about the ending of PhiliPussies.'

'She doesn't care. I think she was getting a bit bored with it, anyway. Apparently she's setting up a new charity to give homes to donkeys from Syria.'

'Oh well, that would figure,' said Mrs Pargeter. 'So you no longer have any involvement with PhiliPussies?'

'I told you, it's closed down. How can I have any involvement in a charity that's closed down?'

'So you're not even involved in the . . . microchipping part of the business?' Mrs Pargeter asked innocently.

Her sister-in-law looked straight at her. She knew exactly what Mrs Pargeter meant, that she was referring to the smuggling of uranium pellets. But she made no comment.

Instead, she said, 'Anyway, at the moment, Melita, it seems that you are in the ascendency in our relationship.'

'That's very nice of you to say so.'

'As I mentioned in my email, we're at an impasse. You have information which, if made public, could ruin me. And I have information which, if made public, could ruin you.'

'Well, I agree with the first part of that statement,' said Mrs Pargeter judiciously. 'But I don't think you have any information on me that wouldn't, if made public, incriminate you as well.'

'How do you work that out?'

'Oh, come on, Rochelle. I've got so much. I've got information that would definitely associate you with the activities of the Lambeth Walkers.'

'And I've got information that would definitely associate you with the activities of my brother.'

'Well, of course, I was married to him.' Mrs Pargeter went on, stating with complete confidence, 'But there's no information out there that would connect my husband to anything criminal.'

Rochelle Brighouse looked deeply frustrated as her sister-in-law continued, 'Whereas I have so many ways of making your life difficult. As I say, it's all chronicled in Tumblers Tate's archive. And then I've got Ellie Fenchurch – you know, the journalist – lined up to do a big Sunday paper exposé on the Lambeth Walkers the minute I say the word.'

Now Rochelle looked frightened. 'And are you about to say the word?'

'Oh goodness, no.' Mrs Pargeter was not a vindictive person. 'I just want you to be aware that, if you cause me any more trouble—' she smiled a sweet smile – 'I can ruin you at a moment's notice.'

'And if I don't "cause you any trouble" . . .'

Mrs Pargeter spread her hands generously wide. 'Then no problems. We can both get on with our own lives.'

'And meet occasionally socially . . . like sister-in-laws do . . .?' Rochelle suggested ironically.

Mrs Pargeter shook her head. 'No, that's never going to work, is it?'

'No.'

Rochelle Brighouse picked up her handbag. 'I think we've probably said everything we have to say to each other.'

'I'd go along with that.'

'And I don't really fancy eating a meal with someone who's blackmailing me.'

'As you like.'

'So I'll say goodbye.'

Rochelle rose from her chair. Neither woman felt inclined even to shake hands. But when she was halfway across the room, Rochelle noticed that her sister-in-law was holding out her right hand, cupped, as if expecting something to be put in it.

Wordlessly, Rochelle Brighouse took something out of her bag and placed it in the waiting hand. It was the late Mr Pargeter's little black book.

Mrs Pargeter never liked anything to go to waste, so she invited Truffler Mason to join her for what was, of course, another excellent dinner.

The book launch was held in the Angolds' new house. Discreet sales of some of the jewellery that Jasmine Angold's late husband had bequeathed to her (via Epping Forest) had raised enough money for her to move from Romford upmarket to Chigwell. She was now a near neighbour of Mrs Pargeter.

It was of course the latter's idea that Charley Angold's memoir of her husband should be published. She found an online service which produced very nice-looking volumes to order. She had to pay for them, of course. It was the new form of vanity publishing, which allowed absolutely anything to appear in book form. And allowed aspirant authors the chance to have a lot of books with their name on piled up in their garages.

Mrs Pargeter had had the book printed, partly because she wanted to have a copy for herself, but also to stop Jasmine Angold wittering on about meeting the demands of her late husband's last letter to his daughter.

Mrs Pargeter had offered to provide the champagne for the launch, but Jasmine, with her new-found wealth, insisted on paying for it herself. The author of the book being celebrated, her daughter Charley, was there of course, accompanied by a relatively new boyfriend. To the surprise of everyone, he actually seemed to be rather nice, and Charley thought she might have to reconsider some of her comments about the inadequacies of the male gender.

Erin was there, of course, but on her own. Her workaholic tendencies still didn't give much opportunity for a boyfriend to get a look-in.

Truffler Mason was present, in his inescapable brown suit, with the beige raincoat over the back of his chair. So was Gary, whose admiring glances Mrs Pargeter continued to be unaware of.

And Parvez the Peterman attended, still bathing in the glow of being acknowledged as the best cracksman in the world.

Untroubled by the crowd, Jasmine Angold's tortoiseshell cat Nana sat on a fur rug in the middle of the room, attended by her two growing kittens, Winsome and Losesome. The three of them could have been auditioning for a job on the front of a chocolate box.

It was an extremely jolly party.

Mrs Pargeter felt very blessed.